From The Women's Press Ltd
124 Shoreditch High Street, London E1

Frankie Finn   *Photo by Pauline Utter*

Frankie Finn was born in Kent and studied English Literature at the University of East Anglia. She then worked as a counsellor/social worker in a number of different contexts, amongst others in a therapeutic community, an adventure playground, a hostel for the physically handicapped and a crisis centre. In 1981 she went to Canada to study for an M.A. in English Literature and Creative Writing at the University of New Brunswick; she now lives in London.

Her play, *Collecting Leaves*, was performed by Mouth and Trousers Theatre Company as part of a Showcase of New Women Writers in 1982, and she has written and performed in several plays in Canada, including one which was commissioned by the Canadian Crafts Council. This is her first novel.

FRANKIE FINN

Out On The Plain

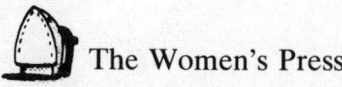 The Women's Press

First published in Great Britain by
The Women's Press Limited 1984
A member of the Namara Group
124 Shoreditch High Street, London E1 6JE

British Library Cataloguing in Publication Data

Finn, Frankie
    Out on the plain
    I. Title
    823'.914 [F] PR6056.I518/

    ISBN 0-7043-2853-4
    ISBN 0-7043-3942-0 Pbk

Typeset by MC Typeset, Chatham, Kent
Printed and bound in Great Britain
by Nene Litho and Woolnough Bookbinding
both of Wellingborough, Northants

To Norma Finn, my mother, my friend:
fellow walker, animated talker,
kindred spirit in sorrow and in laughter . . .
I honour you.

Author's Introduction

The woman on the empty stage is dressed as a clown. She cannot leave the stage. She throws herself about the stage with a desperate rush from gesture to gesture. She holds herself still, poised; her smile is pulled out too long . . . she hears laughter. She has not intended her posture to be amusing. She flees to the wings and comes back dressed as someone else, stepping tight, short steps; she wears a new hat, she gestures timidly; now will I do? She hears laughter, sneering . . . no, she will not do. And then she is angry and now she is kneeling and tearing at her hair . . . and this seems to work; approval is granted for the woman to destroy herself . . . the audience evaporates and she is alone. Her desperate dance has taken place in silence. All the while she has been silent, dumb . . . and this is the prelude to this novel – a dumbshow; a period of entertaining despair in silence . . . She wakes up, in an empty room, on a cold shore, and reaches out her hand and grips the pen. Gripping the pen is an act of faith, for then the words start to come. Slowly, softly, but trickling hope the words start to come . . . the time before spring. She writes in her diary: 'If I write a book, I want to write a lonely, hopeful book.'

That was January 1980, another year passed before I was ready to write my book. I had left university with a degree in English Literature in 1976, thinking how much I despised words. Words and literature are not life, I had decided, and therefore I had written or read very little since. This distinction between literature and life, I now find false, but sitting in the university, as does Helen in *Out On The Plain*, who has not looked out of the window and felt great gaping gulfs between what is being 'studied', what is going on in the street, and what one is feeling inside? So, directing my attentions eagerly towards 'life', I worked for the next four years in various

1

'helping' situations, the last of which was a twenty-four hour 'Crisis and Support' counselling centre. Five staff, five thousand calls a year. Callers went away, refreshed perhaps, determined, consoled, but to be working there involved continuous exposure to fear and pain, which was at times overwhelming. I don't know if 'ordinary life' is, in fact, so full of pain; it seemed so then, except that, like *Wuthering Heights* there was little that was 'ordinary' about it – a steady, passionate flood of sniffles, shrieks and groans – vivid, immediate. What remained of my energy was expended on the dance above, and when the audience, the man I was living with, left, I found myself alone and to myself I had nothing to say. It was as if I had thrown myself away.

I discovered a new yearning for solitude, for scribbling in solitude; the fascination with words had not died. In June 1980 I gave up my job and found the houseboat on the Thames on which I was to live alone for the following year. I started to read again. I read Colette – Colette locked in a room and forced to write. I read *Patterns of Creativity Mirrored in Creation Myths* by Marie Von Franz:

> If you are alone a lot of your life, energy, normally used up in relating to the other things, one could say the whole 'social energy', is suddenly dammed up and has no outlet and therefore flows back into and constellates the unconscious.[1]

I was enchanted by the idea of 'constellation' in the unconscious and by the manifold nature of creation and birth displayed in the myths discussed.

A course on women writers and women's writing was offered by the Workers Educational Association near Stoke-on-Trent. It was a week's course; I went. We were a group of women of mixed ages and backgrounds staying in a converted vicarage in the countryside. It was August and very hot. The food was wonderful. Why bother to mention the food? Because it was unusual. It struck us all at the time that it was very unusual that a motley group of women, such as ourselves, should be gathered together and fed good food. (I think of Virginia Woolf's remarks about the meagre and bland rations sloshed up in the women's colleges in Oxbridge compared to the splendid feasts lavished upon the men.) For us, nourishment of the body combined easily with nourishment of the mind. Together we explored aspects of women's writing (starting, of course, with *A Room of One's Own*), aspects which are the common fare of many women's writing groups: the themes of mothers and daughters, sisters, pregnancy, madness, anger, fear, frustration, silence . . . then, breaking through, rebirth. These are the themes, but what was equally important was the nourishing quality of the talk. There was little judgment, much encouragement, a sharing of personal experience . . . the living of it, the walking and talking with women about women's writing, about our own writing, all day long and into the evening. Being heard.

Back on the boat the period of fruitful solitude began. I was reading avidly now. There was an exhilaration, a sense of purpose in my reading, which I had never had before. Almost all the books I read were written by women. Ranging freely, I discovered in them a sense of identification, a touching, a quality, a tone difficult to define. Sometimes defiant, sometimes offering, these voices carried a certain integrity, a deep concern for truth, a commitment to the throwing off of stale and static forms. Not one voice, not one stance, but a similarity of gesture, for, as Mary Daly says, 'She is many verbs.'[2] This is described by women writers in many ways: 'It's faithfulness I care about' (Anais Nin).

As for my own writing – not only did I feel a new voice in me, but also the need to express myself in a new form. In speculating upon the form a woman writer might choose, Virginia Woolf comments:

> Yet who shall say that now 'the novel' (I give it inverted commas to mark my sense of the word's inadequacy), who shall say that even this most pliable of all forms is rightly shaped for her use? No doubt we shall find her knocking that into shape for herself when she has the free use of her limbs; and providing some new vehicle, not necessarily in verse, for the poetry in her.[3]

The novel I was then drafting about my grandmother, which had begun as a short story, evolved quite spontaneously into a poetic play, *Collecting Leaves*. I continued to read, connections were establishing themselves in my mind, the women's bookshop in Islington became a place of pilgrimage, I went to conferences on women's art. I spent a great deal of time with my women friends. The women from the course in Stoke lived in different parts of the country, but we were all sending letters, poems, ideas to each other. We published a booklet of our work. My play was performed in London as part of 'A Showcase of New Women Writers'. I spent hours and hours with my mother; we talked eagerly, actively developing our relationship, sharing books, ideas, laughing. Both of us were changing. The first big, officially recognised exhibition of women's art was held at the Institute of Contemporary Arts. I went with my friend Praxy, and, when I was wondering if I could afford to buy the catalogue, she said, 'You must, this is important.'

The contribution of women to the arts is still only partially recognised. Academic institutions now entertain it to varying degrees; a token course here and there may be thrown in, but, in my experience at least, such courses tend to be superficial. In 1978 Adrienne Rich was moved to write an essay entitled 'Taking Women Students Seriously'.[4] Much of her comment has gone unheeded. Nevertheless, an article by John Hofsess, 'The Hand That Holds the Pen', begins: 'For a decade now most important contemporary writers have been women.' After mentioning Adrienne Rich, Kate Millett, Nadine Gordimer and others, he continues:

They are serious writers in search of as large an audience as possible, without oversimplifying or pandering. They are not content to be cult writers, or to have no *political* effect. They write to change the world – which is largely a man's world – . . . The modern era has also had its share of gifted male writers, but even the best seem unable to transcend the paltry compulsions of ego and penis; it's as if most male writers of the late 20th century are no longer capable of imagining and desiring a better world, for both sexes, and all races, and are content with perfecting a *style* for their despair and acceptance of viciousness.[5]

4

Gradually the recognition of women's writing *is* growing. The influence of the women's movement is beginning to be felt internationally as a vital political force. I think, for example, of women's contribution to the peace movement and remember the words of Virginia Woolf in *Three Guineas:* 'As a woman I have no country . . . As a woman my country is the whole world.' As Adrienne Rich says: 'The sleepwalkers are coming awake and for the first time awakening has a collective reality, it is no longer such a lonely thing to open one's eyes.'[6]

We have begun to hope that perhaps the isolation, the humiliation of the dumbshow might be over, but in which direction does a woman who wishes to write look when she first opens her eyes? 'A woman writing thinks back through her mothers' (Virginia Woolf, *A Room of One's Own,* p. 96). I found myself looking and 'thinking' back. I reread Jane Austen, George Eliot and Charlotte Brontë with curiosity, focusing now on what these women writers were expressing about being women, looking in fact for where they deviate from, rather than conform to, the canon of English Literature. I came to reverence these writers as women of courage who valued their own sex. I had always felt a strong sympathy for them but now I began to understand it more precisely. With what delight I read George Eliot's comment in *Middlemarch* on Dorothea's hands: 'They were not thin hands; but powerful, feminine, maternal hands.' Dorothea, Emma, Lucy Snowe are not pretty women. (In fact each is played off against a woman who is more the stereotype – Rosamund, Harriet, Paulina.) They are struggling with aspirations and feelings unaccommodated by the society which surrounds and threatens to engulf them. In portraying strong, intelligent, conventionally unattractive women, these writers are being subversive. But Ellen Morgan is one of many feminist critics who makes the following point in relation to the heroines: 'Her efforts to acquire a philosophy of life and the art of living were stunted when they began to imply real rebellion and social alienation.'[7] Eventually, their brave and creative vision is stifled.

Mothers?

I had a dream of nourishment
Against a breast
My infant face was presst   (Stevie Smith)

Mothers? Where are the women in history? Silence. Of course, I could discern the occasional presence – a witch burning here and there, or a crown begrudgingly placed on a female head when there was no man around to claim it, even a few words like 'Let them eat cake!' But I could not *feel* their influence. Women 'appear' in history as they 'appear' in other male products; in paintings and in literature. They do not, however, act or contribute. There is an eerie quality to their silence; it is unnatural.

I read *The First Sex, The Descent of Woman* and *The Paradise Papers*, books which are concerned with the history of women; gradually, the woman writer thinking back through her mothers comes to understand and is profoundly shocked by the extent to which, and the vicious means by which, her mothers have been silenced. When I was ready (for I knew it would be a difficult, painful and challenging book), I read Mary Daly's *Gyn/Ecology*. In this book, at great length and in careful detail, Mary Daly scrutinises the motivation and methodology behind the ritualistic practice of violence, both physical and psychological, which has been and is still being perpetrated against women throughout the world. Mary Daly is encouraging an anger, a fire. We have a right to be angry, but she is also nurturing a listening, a hope. For if we can squeeze under and around the grim assumptions of history which stand like a portcullis guarding the past, eventually we rediscover a life-affirming principle concealed in the lost civilisations of the matriarchs and the myths of the Goddess. I sat back in the boat. Goddess? I read that in the oldest Creation myth the earth was not manufactured by a male god but given birth to by the Goddess Tiamat; that it was the Goddess Nidaba, Scribe of the Sumerian heaven, who was worshipped as the first patron deity of writing. Yes, Goddess. The effort needed to understand seemed impossible. I was having to face an unspeakable pain of alienation. Although everything I had come to realise was contradicted by the bustle of 'life' I could see carrying on as usual about me, I had come to believe in the invisible. That was frightening, and what was more frightening was that deep down I had known about this all along.

After I had been writing for several months it became clear that I would have to find some form of financial support if I were to continue. In September 1981 I left for Canada where I studied literature and creative writing at the University of New Brunswick; I was given a small grant and the opportunity to finish my work. I read more. Perhaps I should make it clear that I am not claiming that it is only women who have cause to challenge society. There have, of course, always been challengers, women and men, and there are often links between the many routes of challenge; but feminism is the route I take because it affects my life so deeply that, in fact, I have no choice. When one ceases to apply patriarchal values to history, the importance of laws and wars diminishes as the relevance of women's occupations such as nursing, midwifery, childrearing, the provision of food, weaving and spinning becomes more apparent. In literature, exciting discoveries are made. I discover that the first book in the English language and the first autobiography were both written by women. But the process is dialectical, for each discovered fragment serves to emphasise the immensity of the loss. I listen, for instance, to Sappho:

> A company of horsemen or of infantry
> Or a fleet of ships, some say,
> Is the black earth's finest sight,
> But to me it is what you love.[8]

Or to the lonely voice of Christine de Pisan, a contemporary of Chaucer, who says of women:

> They murder no one, nor wound, nor harm,
> Betray men, nor pursue, nor seize
> Nor houses set on fire, nor disinherit men,
> Nor poison, nor steal gold or silver. . .[9]

Or to Amelia Lanier, a contemporary of Shakespeare, who speaks on behalf of women in a poem dedicated to her friend, Mary Sidney:

> Then let us have our Liberty again,
> And challenge to yourselves no Sovereignty;
> You came not in the world without our pain,
> Make that a bar against your cruelty;[10]

These words gather and form a kind of chanting echo through history, 'a sense of wrong voiced', as Tillie Olsen puts it in *Silences*.

Carol Christ, in her book, *Diving Deep and Surfacing: Women Writers on Spiritual Quest,* points to the vital dialectic of story-telling:

> Stories give shape to experience, experience gives rise to stories. . . The dialectic between experience and shaping experience through story-telling has not been in women's hands. Instead of recognizing their own experiences, giving names to their feelings, and celebrating their perceptions of the world, women have often suppressed and denied them.[11]

A woman wishing to tell her story in the twentieth century, who has managed to find a room of her own and money to support her, will need certain tools; pen, paper – and language. She then encounters a problem, for the words and language available to her are also the tools of a system which seeks to undermine her. I think of the words associated with woman . . . spinster, hussy, whore, cunt, tit, bitch, hag, tart. The synonyms for 'womanish' are listed in my *Thesaurus* as follows: 'effeminate, emasculated, unmanly, cowardly, shrill, vixenish, soft, weak. Antonym: see Male courage.' From this one might easily infer that there is no such thing as female courage! The inference is incorrect; it is not female courage which is lacking but the word for it. Look at the difference in the pictures conjured up by the words 'hero' and 'heroine'! In *Man Made Language,* Dale Spender explores the subtle means by which language condemns,

8

negates and incriminates women, she shows how women are persistently taught to think of themselves as lesser than, or the other side of male. She points out, for example, that the sexual act is assimilated purely in terms of male perception, thus we are taught to talk of 'penetration' but not 'enclosure'. Sometimes a women will find herself wrongly labelled under a male term: I have a degree in English Literature and thus am referred to as a Bachelor of Arts, although I think of myself as a Spinster of Arts, which surely is more correct. Sometimes she will find herself semi-included which causes confusion: in *A Glossary of Literary Terms* (a work which I am led to believe concerns itself with accuracy and with the precise definition of language) I read:

EMPATHY . . . Empathy . . . signifies an experience in which *one* identifies *himself* with an object of perception and seems to participate in its physical sensations.

This 'one' has difficulty in knowing whether she is included or not. Moreover, this 'one' seems to have developed a sudden, strange distrust for 'empathy', and it also appears to this 'one' that language is somewhat 'one-sided', and if, as the above indicates, 'one' equals 'him', language is 'himsided'. This 'one' is then brought to ask herself if she, in fact, exists. She turns to Dale Spender for reassurance:

Many, many feminist writers who have tried to articulate the difficulties encountered in trying to encode feminist reality have also, directly and indirectly, referred to the phenomenon of being confined to the words of the dominant group, and 'having to tell our truths in an alien language' (Rich).[12]

What happens? I get angry and when I am angry I can't write or speak, the attempt and the desire to communicate breaks down, I retreat to the kitchen and the dirty dishes. And if it seems to you reading this that the hand holding the pen is not quite as even-tempered as is thought desirable, and if at times you can detect a tone which could be termed 'shrill' or 'vixenish', it is because of the anger which I have to keep dampening down! Virginia Woolf finds herself in a similar predicament when writing *A Room of One's Own* and wastes a morning:

> Anger had snatched my pencil while I dreamt. But what was anger doing there? . . . it was the professor's statement about the mental, moral and physical inferiority of women. My heart leapt. My cheek burnt. I had flushed with anger. There was nothing specially remarkable, however foolish, in that. One does not like to be told that one is naturally the inferior of a little man – I looked at the student next to me – who breathes hard, wears a ready-made tie and has not shaved for a fortnight (p. 33).

This anger, this ever-smouldering and readily combustible feeling of outrage, is so draining on the woman writer, the 'sense of wrong voiced'. Mary Daly reconverts words. Unearthing their origins, she restores to words like spinster, crone, hag, a power and a strength, a dignity, a wisdom: 'Hags may rage and roar,' she says, 'but they do not titter.' I feel better.

Back to the beginning, and the winter on the boat. I went through a tremendous period of spiritual activity. I was living so vividly or, rather, seeing so vividly. For through all the anger and the pain, a vision was shaping. My vocabulary was changing. Words like truth, beauty, faith, tenderness, sacred, spinning, and weaving . . . I was beginning to trust and reclaim them. The women writers met again. We were all moving; our poems shared images, tones, which had not been conspicuous before. Returning from a weekend we spent together, I wrote in my diary:

> There is a certain quality which is achieved only by having a group of women together . . . a lateralness, a nowness. Tiny, tiny sprinkles of hope, freshness . . . and what is so sacred now is life and the patterns of life and the colours of life and not the dull grey lines. I think I'm beginning to move into another sphere . . .

and I think of the things I see (imagine) . . . women on a shore picking up jewels, a cold dawn, muddy landscape, alone like animals are alone together, in a herd or a pack, capable of flight if necessary. This is blue and yellow. What is happening? It seems like I am creating my own landscape inside my head . . . I must go there often and think about this landscape. Fight the straight lines!

This discovery of a shared and imaginatively accessible female landscape was later to be borne out by my reading of contemporary writers such as Susan Griffin and Marge Piercy. In Monique Wittig's *Les Guérillères* there is a declared resistance to convenient or conventional definition:

The women say that they perceive their bodies in their entirety. They say that they do not favour any of its parts on the grounds that it was formerly a forbidden object. They say that they do not want to become prisoners of their own ideology. They say that they do not garner and develop the symbols that were necessary to them at an earlier period to demonstrate their strength. For example they do not compare the vulvas to the sun moon and stars. They do not say that the vulvas are like black suns in the shining night.[13]

Monique Wittig has travelled much further than I have into uncharted country; at times I find her writing disturbingly anarchic; at others I am amazed and strengthened by the similarities.

In January 1981 I was reading Virginia Woolf's journals, Katherine Mansfield's letters. Visions, dreams, quotations, snatches of anger . . . I jotted them all down in my diary. I was starting to think seriously about my craft. Travelling up to London on the train, looking out of the window, wondering furiously . . . what is the word for this? What is the phrase for that? Living on the water, I described my state of mind as 'torn but exulting'. Increasingly, in the work of the women I was reading, entwining amongst the 'sense of wrong voiced', I could hear a voice hopefully replenishing. In February I began the first draft of *Out On The Plain*.

I wanted to write a hopeful book. Just as the tone and meaning of certain words were beginning to settle and unfold in my mind, so my ideas of form and style were developing. My ideas mostly evolved through my reading of literature. However, similar concerns are to be found amongst women working in other areas. In a discussion shared by five women involved in the visual arts published under the title 'What is Female Imagery?' the art critic Lucy Lippard makes a distinction which I find particularly significant:

> Of course, 'female imagery' was first used, and should continue to be used, to mean female *sexual* imagery . . . I prefer 'female sensibility' . . . There is a lot of sexual imagery in women's art – circles, domes, eggs, spheres, boxes, biomorphic shapes, maybe a certain striation or layering. But that's too specific. It's more interesting to think about fragments, which imply a certain antilogical, antilinear approach also common to many women's work.[14]

In her essay in *Woman as Writer,* Joanna Russ says:

> There seem to me to be two alternatives open to the woman author who no longer cares about How She Fell in Love or How She Went Mad. These are (1) lyricism and (2) life.

She defines lyricism as follows:

> . . . the principle of construction I wish to call *lyric* consists in the *organisation of discrete elements* (images, events, scenes, passages, words, what-have-you) around an *unspoken thematic or emotional center.* The lyric mode exists without chronology or causation, its principle is *associative.*[15]

I cannot pretend that I sat myself down forthwith to write a 'lyric novel of female sensibility!' I had not even read these comments at the time. Nevertheless, I think they are helpful indicators of the method employed in writing *Out On The Plain.*

The lyric mode flowered in this century in the work of Virginia

Woolf, but its roots go back, beyond the restrictive chronological rules imposed on literature by Aristotle, to Sappho, and back to the mimetic chants and hymns sung by the women in the temples of the Goddess, to the genesis of art. Sappho's poetry is alive with sensation, with freshness and flowers:

> All yellow, gold like a daughter,
> A flower, that girl, with a flower's beauty.

It has the direct clarity and grace of Chaucer or even Shakespeare. It combines laughter and sadness; it is a celebration of the complexity of life. In the introduction in my copy of her work I read that Sappho's poetry 'belongs to cultural springtime and renaissances'[16] and that 'Neither Sappho nor Botticelli separated beauty from intelligence' (p. 10). I think there is a connection here; the lyrical quality which is emerging in some women's work *is* associated with springtime and renaissance, the recovery of colourful life. It seeks to recombine beauty and intelligence, not impose meanings, nor sever life from death. It is dedicated to a sort of active receptivity, to wholeness, to the principles of life and hope, and, considering the destruction and devastation so rampant in the world today, it is a matter of urgency that we listen to it.

If anger inhibits a woman writer from realising the true extent of her vision – so also does fear. I experience tremendous difficulties in preserving faith. A phenomenon which most, probably all, women writers are aware of and in one way or another respond to, is the voice of male censure, both inside and outside. It is the censure which has shaped our lives, the male audience we have been taught to please, the authoritative weight of literature, the lover who applauds our gestures as victim. Of course, there is something wrong with the words one chooses – beauty? truth? faithfulness? – out of date, mawkish, precious. Of course, to write about one's own experience is to be self-indulgent, nagging, boring, limited. Of course, 'domestic imagery' is of minimal significance. Of course, women's talk is trifling, hysterical, emotional, vague, unrealistic

... OK, sometimes it can be entertaining, ornamental, but not much else. Of course . . . this is what goes on inside, and, of course, I am frightened, I stumble and of course I get angry; for our oppression has been internalised. Virginia Woolf named this phenomenon 'the lash on the shoulder'. Emily Dickinson talks of 'telling it slant', Honor Moore the 'Male Approval Desire . . . abbreviated M.A.D.' So, when a woman picks up her pen feeling that she has something she wishes to express, she is going to be WRONG or M.A.D. or both. And in walked Mr Smith-god and Mr Jones just like that! Mr Smith-god and Mr Jones are supposed to be stereotypes or perhaps, more accurately, a composite legion of stereotypes. The struggle with them, however, is real. I am fortunate that they lack humour. Jane Austen, George Eliot, Charlotte Brontë and Virginia Woolf all use humour to defuse anger whilst at the same time making a point. I follow their example. Another way in which I can cope with Mr Smith-god and Mr Jones is in the imagery which surrounds them. Mr Jones's fear of spontaneous life is indicated by his slavish obsession with pinpricks and pedantry, 'the engrossing task of killing very small things slowly'. Mr Smith-god is always rearing his head up all over the place, but the accent is on deflation. They are easy to write about. I have to be very careful, because they are so 'up-front' and familiar, that their role of comic relief does not trick us into finding them endearing and thus obscure the vicious, self-righteous motivation of their actions.

In *Out On The Plain*, I have invested a great deal in the reader/writer relationship. Women's writing is not just the 'big four' (Austen, Eliot, Brontë and Woolf). Much of women's writing is to be found in letters and journals; it is born out of talking; it has an oral tradition. I therefore use the first person and the present tense. I think the active, creative potential of reading is devalued in our society; we seem to ignore or do not respect the obvious fact that words on a page are first of all words on a page – an arrangement of lines and squiggles on a sheet of paper – and their life depends on being read.

As I hope to show with the introduction of Helen into the novel, I soon began to feel dissatisfied with the cosy reader/writer relationship I had set up in the beginning. It was proving to be idealistic, simplistic and bossy. My intention to have an open relationship with an unknown reader was working against itself: for you can't really have much of a discussion with an unknown reader, what you start doing is to make assumptions about her, and this dilemma Helen forces me to face. Her claim that she, as reader and character, has a right to some input into the story is healthy. Her distrust of my feminism is likewise healthy; she brings me down to earth. Throughout, she provides me with opportunities to disagree with and make fun of myself, which I hope has the effect of relaxing and humanising the tone. Helen's distrust of my attitude is also based on a real fear and feeling of loss, which is inevitable when one turns one's back on the system of belief with which one is familiar, to venture off into the unknown. In choosing the society of women, Virginia Woolf says in a letter, 'Men are in the light always, with women you swim at once into the silent dusk.' There are times when I, like Helen, find this frightening.

I had put myself into a precarious position of physical isolation, alone on a boat which often came close to sinking, from which I was confronting a silence in history, a silence in myself, and a blank sheet of paper. But, in her poem 'Cartographies of Silence', Adrienne Rich says:

> Silence can be a plan
> rigorously executed
>
> the blueprint to a life
>
> It has a presence
> it has a history a form
>
> Do not confuse it
> with any kind of absence[17]

Because women do not, by and large, belong to the organisations of power in this society, they are thought to be 'good listeners'. 'Is there any connection between the devaluation of women and the devaluation of listening?' asks Dale Spender. We live in a world which does not listen, answers are supplied before questions are

15

asked; words are devalued. I wished to adopt a listening attitude, listening rather than imposing, open rather than closed. It is necessary to listen, to others, to oneself, before one speaks. Some time after I had begun to write, I was in a storytelling workshop at a matriarchy conference where we did precisely this; women sitting in a circle listening to silence. In such activity there is no contradiction; for in recognising the power of our silence, the gentle determination to create is restored.

Notes

1. Marie-Louise Von Franz, *Patterns of Creativity Mirrored in Creation Myths*, Zurich, Spring Publications, 1978, p. 119.
2. Mary Daly, *Gyn/Ecology: The Metaethics of Radical Feminism*, London, The Women's Press, 1979, p. xii.
3. Virginia Woolf, *A Room of One's Own*, Harmondsworth, Penguin, 1972, pp. 77–8.
4. Adrienne Rich, *On Lies, Secrets and Silence: Selected Prose 1966–1978*, London, Virago, 1980, pp. 237–45.
5. John Hofsess, 'The Hand That Holds the Pen', *Books in Canada*, 12, no. 2 (Feb. 1983), p. 12.
6. From 'When We Dead Awaken: Writing as Revision', in *On Lies, Secrets and Silence, op. cit.*, p. 35.
7. Ellen Morgan, 'Humanbecoming: Form and Focus in the Neo-Feminist Novel', in *Feminist Criticism: Essays on Theory, Poetry and Prose*, Cheryl L. Brown and Karen Olson, eds., Methuen, N.J., Scarecrow Press, 1978, p. 273.
8. Guy Davenport, trans., *Archilochos: Sappho: Alkman*, Berkeley, University of California Press, 1980.
9. Christine de Pisan, *Oeuvres Poétiques*, 3 vols., ed. Maurice Roy, Paris, 1965, vol. 2, p. 21, as cited in Frances and Joseph Gies, *Women in the Middle Ages*, London, Barnes and Noble, 1980, p. 11.
10. Amelia Lanier, *Salve Deus Rex Judaeorum*, London, printed by V. Simmes for R. Bonian, 1611; as cited in Mary R. Mahl and Helene Koon, eds., *The Female Spectator*, New York, The Feminist Press, 1977, p. 86.
11. Carol P. Christ, *Diving Deep and Surfacing: Women Writers on Spiritual Quest*, Boston, Beacon Press, 1980, p. 5.
12. Dale Spender, *Man Made Language*, London, Routledge and Kegan Paul, 1980, p. 83.
13. Monique Wittig, *Les Guérillères*, London, The Women's Press, 1979, pp. 57–8.
14. Lucy Lippard, 'What is Female Imagery?' in *From the Center*, New York, E. P. Dutton, 1976, p. 81.
15. Joanna Russ, 'What Can a Heroine Do? or Why Women Can't Write', in *Woman as Writer*, Jeannette L. Webber and Joan Grumman, eds., Boston, Houghton Mifflin, 1978, p. 158.
16. Guy Davenport, *op.cit.*, p. 5.
17. Adrienne Rich, 'Cartographies of Silence', in *The Dream of a Common Language: Poems 1974–1977*, New York, W. W. Norton, 1978, p. 17.

Out On The Plain

Before Beginning

Give it back to me!
The cold space of a February afternoon is ripped open.
Give me back my pen!

Was it my screaming which brought you here? No, not
initially . . . you could not have heard my cries until you were
already close. Did you see alarm in the hot black smoke rushing out
of my fragile chimney pipe? No, it is too quickly absorbed by the
mass of blank air which hangs above and waits patiently, to darken
into the Thames. Or perhaps it was just an idle moment in which
your curious hand lifted the cover of this book, that led you to step
out of the main street into the narrow alley between the Bingo Hall
and the cafe and so discover yourself in the boatyard.

I don't see you come. It is my cat, by nature attentive and helpful,
who first observes you. She sits on the roof, watching, as you pick
your way slowly over the rickety gang planks amongst the old
houseboats which huddle grimly to the bank and through the yard
where rubbish stands in still piles and the rusty wheelbarrow rusts
solitary on the disused slipway . . .

Let go of my pen! Sorry, I was not speaking to you, you who the
cat on the roof observes.

You thread yourself under the electricity wires which droop
across the concrete. You approach my boat. I know it doesn't look
like a boat; more like a long, green floating shed with its flat roof
. . . but the battered stem of a chimney and the dashes of the bright
tartan material at the edges of eight square windows give it a
homely, gypsy air. The river is low, before the turning of the tide, so
that the windows are level with the bank; you squat down in order
to peer in.

There is no light on. You adjust your vision through a cobweb and your own reflection and you see a sideboard, then an empty chair, a small table covered with a lace cloth, a vase of flowers, a stack of books, things as they are . . . positioned or left about. I am sitting in my chair beside the woodburning stove with my pen gripped in my hand, my writing pad is balanced on my knees, my head down; position thoughtful, concentrating, furtive. Two large hands rise out of the gloom beneath the window and snap the curtains shut; they are not my hands.

When and if, when and if . . . you jump down, you are inside, entering the little sitting-room. The rocking room is rocking gloom, dim apart from the flickering of the stove. It appears that I am alone. Water is slapping against the side.

Thank you, thank you so much for coming. I note down the way in which you hesitate, then take off your coat and place your bag beside you. You sit on the edge of the visitor's chair and wait. Of course, I feel guilty that you have bothered to come at all, I have nothing to offer you except this vague idea for a book. I have been longing for a woman to talk to. Minutes pass, I draw a little picture of you in my margin . . . Would you like a cup of tea?

Pen and pad in hand, I get up, step around the stove and leave the room. Safe in the kitchen, I clatter about with the tin tray and the sugar bowl and the biscuit barrel, cups chinking and the water in the kettle rising merrily to the boil, whilst you perch on the edge of your chair and wait beside the flowers on the table, daffodils; timid beams of yellow. You watch the light around the base of the stove, flexing back and forth across the white carpet . . . but something is not right, there is something ominous, odd . . . and then . . . and then your attention is arrested by the twinkling tips of two highly polished black boots peeking out from under the dark red curtain which divides off an area behind the stove. Looking up slowly, you discern that there is a large bulge in the curtain above the boots . . . that, indeed, someone is wearing the boots and that someone is concealed behind the curtaining . . . I return from the kitchen, clutching my pad and my pen against the side of the tray. I set them down carefully on the table and pour us a cup of tea.

You see, I begin again, leaning back in my chair . . .

'Ahem, ahem. . . .' I am interrupted by a sort of thrashing movement behind the red curtain, and then, with a ceremonious thrust, the curtain is swept aside, and there, stiffened before us, beneath quantities of billowing grey robes, stands Mr Smith-god himself. Don't let us recoil in fear, such as is expected of us . . . don't let us abandon each other to make him feel comfortable . . . I mutter to you under my breath . . . But now, grave and flaring, Mr Smith-god strides into the little room, long white locks streaming behind him, like one who strides across a golf course. The room is tiny. He halts behind me with a click of his polished heels. I freeze. Creepy feeling in the back of my neck. His presence leans and towers over me; a disturbance in the air as he raises his hammer with a jolly swing . . . and pauses, hammer poised above my head; he bares an excessively formal smile in your direction, as if he were expecting you to take a photograph of us, the authors, later to appear on the back cover of this book. When the hammer falls, it hurts.

'You must begin a novel with the words . . . let me see . . . Ahem.' He clears his throat and continues, whacking the words into my head in measured, marching pace. 'The aeroplane burst into flames and fell to the sea. Walter ordered another double brandy. "Such is life!" he remarked to the waitress. "Have a drink on me".'

On the final stroke of the hammer, denoting a full stop, he bends over me and, swiping my pen up from the table, proceeds to pace around the room, robes swishing. His face assumes the expression of 'one lost in profound thought'.

'Give them something solid,' he declares, spinning round on his heel. 'A bit of action! Huh! Trap your audience. Bombard them. Pearls of wisdom.' The phrase 'pearls of wisdom' appears to have particular appeal to him, and he conducts the points of its syllables through the air with the nib of my pen. 'Pearls of wisss . . . ,' up he rises on the tips of his toes . . . All of a sudden he has caught sight of himself in the mirror on the wall and, resting his hammer on the shelf, inclines himself forward like one in a dream to regard his own reflection. He has forgotten all about us and words, he peruses his own image minutely, twirling strands of his moustache fondly, around my pen.

The situation is familiar; all these robes and fluttering locks are blocking the space between us. I have to lean, almost out of my chair to see you in the visitor's chair; we are silent. My hands tremble with frustration around my cup of tea, conversation is difficult and writing is so often a tightly constructed affair which doesn't allow for loop holes and cracks like talking. It is true that the written word may very well produce hard, concentrated little 'pearls of wisdom'. Little pearls . . . something solid to work with, pearls earnestly extracted from the ocean by the deep sea diver, pearls spread out in the palm of the dealer's hand; the perfect pearls and the flawed pearls, the pearls of great worth destined one day for the crowns of kings and queens, the lesser pearls the appropriate adornment for the engagement ring of your friend's sister. But, I'm not diving off the side of the boat to pursue some tiny treasure in the murky depths, neither am I sitting here, crouching over my stove with a pair of tweezers and a bunsen burner, busily employed in polishing, refining . . . I offer you no pearls . . .

'You digress; she isn't interested in that sort of talk!' He struts into position behind me, again the hammer pounds on to my head. 'You must begin a novel with . . . "The aeroplane burst into flames".'

We have had enough. I snatch my pen out of his grasp; the hammer falters. He stomps out of the room, slamming the door . . . a loud dull splash . . . the pursuit of pearls.

I slide open the curtains from across the window. It has started to rain. Rain bounces on to the surface of the water in millions of drops . . . and showers up in tiny fragments, away and up. The pale light is departing swiftly now, but the air, for a moment, lifting fractionally above the row of winter trees on the other side of the river, allows through a few long streaks of gold. The trees are solid. Their black branches stretch up, thickly tangled like pubic hair . . . strong shapes opening their fringes to gold. Behind them the light ebbs away and for a second we see each tree holding her own light; we see her fingering, her pain, her glory . . . the day is gone.

Tapping on the window pane, tapping on the door, insistent, annoying, tap, tap, tapping. Wearily, I go to let the tapper in. I suffer him to follow me, bowing and dripping along the hall into the sitting-room. Mr Jones is very thin and damp.

'Mr Jones,' he says to you; shooting a limp hand in your direction, he winces waiting for it to be shaken. 'Don't mind me,' he says, setting down his briefcase in the corner. He crouches over it and arranges a selection of little tools, devices and instruments on to the carpet; the possibility of our having a conversation is delicately unhinged. He doesn't look very menacing, does he? But we must be wary of one so anxious to please, the eager and youthful intellectual type with the very pointed nose, pointed fingers and a fondness of points in general.

'Don't mind me,' he repeats, commencing to unravel a coil of thin wire. Mr Jones has a very meagre life which he leads out from his bedsit each morning to catch the number 81 bus to his place of work . . . a university perhaps. He spends his day in the office with the door shut tight, his body tensed over structures of words: the sentence and the phrase. With his pen he spears and stabs at words he doesn't like, words which fly, words which swim. When he has killed a word, he pauses to watch its life run out, bleeding colour down the page.

'Excuse me,' he pipes up from beneath my chair where he is attaching his wire to the underside of the upholstery . . . he crawls away behind the stove. What is he doing? He is doing his job, he is laying little traps to catch me out. Traps which I will set off accidentally with the touch of a toe. The toe touches a button, hidden under the carpet, the button pulls the wire tied below the chair, the wire distends a bow, hooked beside the stove and . . . ping, a little arrow glances against my chest . . .

'It works!' Mr Jones claps his hands and flees, work done for the day, to the bus stop. Sitting safely installed on the bus, two seats from the front with his briefcase at his side, Mr Jones smiles. He smiles the sort of smile which squeaks out from between pursed lips, the false smile, the lying kiss.

The stove crackles and flickers. They have gone. I pour us a fresh cup of tea and I ask you to come with me, not only to help fend off Mr Smith-god and Mr Jones . . . but also to share and talk, to laugh, to sing. The daffodils on the table relax their beams and glow boldly golden; the houseboat rocks gently into the lap of the evening.

23

Beginning

Evening. As we sit here opposite one another, two women in the semi-darkness, I find the courage to tell you of my vision.

The darkness is not the beginning. There is a power behind the darkness like the power behind an old, old story which has not been spoken for many years now. Because the story has not been spoken for so long, if we happen to hear its voices whispering, we ignore them; and at evening, if we glimpse a form behind the darkness, we consider it as only a shadow of the darkness. But this is wrong, for the darkness is the shadow; the vision, the power, the story came first.

I stand by the window, looking out. Through the cloaking dusk on the river I see her shape. I cannot see the features in her shape as I cannot see the features in your shape, etched in the darkness of this room. My vision clarifies; her shape is outlined by a bright point of light which rises as a voice exalting rises, swiftly into the atmosphere. I follow the point of light as it ascends, straight above the world. High up, it turns to form the bend of a shoulder and slowly it traces on, up around the curves of a head, then runs along the ridge of another shoulder and falls back down to meet the shadow of the earth. The shape of the early power, the shape of an old, old woman sitting with the darkness of the world folded in her lap.

The coming of evening; the old woman in the sky opens her lap to create a pool of darkness, as she has done over and over again since the beginning of this world. All things of water, earth, and then air, she coaxes, teases with long and gentle fingers, to the rim of the pool. And the elements pause, clutching the creatures which inhabit them, at the brink. They tip over the edge, the fish, the mole, the

24

bird set free, flashing then disappearing into the life of the night. Behind them, the places of habitation; the weeds, the nests, the little houses, are drawn down also, tumbling round and down, as if into the centre of an inverted tornado. And when the last stream of light which composed this day has been dipped from the sky into the dark, and when all the moments have spluttered and expired from the surface of the pool, the arms of the old woman curve softly around her lap, encircling the darkness in a pale ring of silence. It is dark.

. . .

The houseboat sinks steadily through the folds of the night. There is a blood red energy pulsing here in the darkness, expanding and contracting matter and spirit; it is chewing us down, it diminishes our size. Around us, voices, women's voices, lost and angry, crying . . . crying out. Cries fusing in the ferment of the dark.

'I am shut in a cave beneath a rock.'

'I am being beaten in a box behind a waterfall.'

'I am spun along a crevice by a rush of cold air.'

We come to rest like two particles of earth under the weight of a moving mountain. Cramped, in the core of darkness, we sit in our chairs and wait. Before us, fibres of matter, specks of sound, are combining into a substance new and delicate. We watch as a shimmer of hope swells into a bubble of possibility, which begins to rise, bursts and is gone.

And calm settles through the intensity of the darkness. No sound, no light, no voice, no form. Nothing comes and nothing comes and nothing comes . . . until, high in the sky, the old woman who sits with the darkness of the world in her open lap, stretches her back. From her shoulders her body begins to sway.

In the depths, a frail response; an effort. I see a fragile circle is evolving; a circle luminous, like the visible beginnings of a ring of thought. Lost voices weave together in a circumference of whispered sound. We have hands. Hands, women's hands, many and few, many and few, are dancing a flickering circle, tiny, flamelike in the thickest dark. Our hands are kindling the element at the centre of the circle; it softens and clears. Now I see clearly, I see we are many women, we are holding the circle, flat and pale. We lift up the circle, weightless, above our heads, we release it and watch it slide smoothly beautiful as an ordered breath, spiralling a tunnel up through the density of the dark.

The old woman looks down at a small glow which is gradually emerging from the depths of the pool in her lap; it punctures the surface and many shadows filter out, in the manner of a thought being born into consciousness.

· · ·

My vision disappears, suddenly. We have shrunk back into the dark room of the houseboat. I remove the lid from the stove, the embers have sunk down low. I set another log amongst them and replace the lid.

'When I was a little girl,' you say, 'my mother used to read to me when she put me to bed. Sometimes she would close the book in the middle of a story, tuck me in, switch out the light and go downstairs. Then, I would screw my eyes together in the dark and scream and scream until I heard her coming upstairs again, and when I heard her turning the handle on my bedroom door, I would open my eyes and beg her to go on with the story.'

Your poor mother! Did that happen every night?

'No, because I discovered that if I screwed my eyes up really tight I could make it so dark that it became light again and then I could see into the story myself.'

· · ·

We see a grey surface of land spreading away from us, totally flat. No longer dark, not yet light, empty, empy space, not years, not miles. We are shadowy shapes, standing with the shapes of many, many women on the vast expanse of a barren plain, beyond the darkness, our hair blowing in the wind.

And now, sharp as life and brilliant, straight along the horizon, slips a line of liquid energy, a crack which cuts open the earth and throws up a glimmer of pure light. We see the shape of a bare tree before us, beside the crack. At the foot of the tree sits the tiny figure of the old woman. Silence.

26

'But I can hear a voice,' you say.

We listen. The old woman speaks to us. 'Breathe into the emptiness, sisters, and what you breathe out is not emptiness, but flowering life across the plain.'

Towards the tree women are moving forward. Out across the early silence our footprints stretch like lace upon the earth. Whispering, our shadow voices drift and sway in the grey air around us.

'If I were alone, I would be frightened.'

'If you were not here . . .'

'If we chose, we could go back now.'

'I could unravel and roll up my trail like a thread . . .'

'Pop it into the sewing box . . .'

'Snap down the lid.'

'The new light, before light would dwindle and go out. The plain, the tree were never there.'

We join hands. Carefully now, together we raise a foot . . . print. Raise foot . . . print. Each rising up higher, each setting down steadier. We are gathering momentum like a strong wind growing across the waste. With a grunt and a growl we break into a run . . . to run, to run, to run towards. Shall we make music?

'As yet we are too indistinct . . .'

'Shapes and whispers speckling . . .'

'Towards the golden crack . . .'

'Which is quiet and knows where it is going . . .'

'Where the tree grows.'

'And the old woman sits . . .'

But I long to cry out with you, sisters, parts of my soul . . . Hurray! See how we can storm and roar towards the dawn, across the blankness of the page!

'But your voice is only an evening murmur.'

'Your shape, a shadow amongst many who faintly print the trail . . .'

The whispering subsides. In the still dark I turn to you in the visitor's chair. I turn and offer my feeble, yearning emptiness, and my pen hovers frantically, nervous as a bird above the white sheet. For the words which have the power to impress the silence must be

27

hers, the new old woman, the image maker. The boat rocks. Silence mingles. Then, out across the black of night, a steady wave presses homewards and breaks, draining into the greyness of the plain, where our shadows gather under the tree beside the crack. The old woman lifts her head and speaks:

'Sit down, sisters, and make yourselves comfortable on the earth.' As we sit, so the silence folds up her body also and settles herself down with us to listen.

'When you picked up your knife in the kitchen this afternoon and inserted it into the little hole in the fish to make a slit, you smelt the smell of the sea. And for a fragment of a second you lost consciousness of the noise of the children upstairs playing with their toy trains. You ceased, for an instant, to listen for the sound of the car wheel on the gravel drive, your husband coming home. You allowed yourself to let go of the sounds which move your afternoon forward into evening and the television. You pierced the skin of the fish which gave you the smell of the sea in which your aloneness is to be found . . . and looking up, suddenly, out of the window, you knew the early belonging, for there in its full circle of significance before you, you saw the tree . . .'

· · ·

I'm sorry, I can't tell you any more, I say, at last. But when the old woman speaks, each shadow shape hears something different, neither does she hear it at the same time nor in the same place, and as each perfect ring of words is given, so it is broken by the next . . .

You are not listening. You are watching a ray of light which has just splashed out of the stove on to the floor. 'I'll have to go,' you say.

The cat stretches up from her cushion and leaves the room abruptly. The room is very small, the ceiling low. You put on your coat, disturbing the cluttering shadows.

· · ·

Once more there is a breeze running through our hair. We are standing with the many shadows at a distance from the crack, looking towards it. We watch as the first gentle waves of colour

28

begin carefully to permeate the landscape. An arc of soft violet shoots up high into the sky and closes behind us like the hood of an enormous eye. The earth spreads pale and yellow. Yellow which intensifies towards the crack, drips over the edge and flows with the liquid energy in a twisting horizontal line, until finally it meets the faint blue sea. Where the crack touches the sea, the yellow flows into blue and turns to green.

'That's better!' you say.

The tree stands firm in front of the crack, and beyond, beyond the crack, there is nothing but still grey, early mist into which our vision, our colour, cannot penetrate. As we stand in silence, wondering about this, from across the yellow distance of the land we hear the echo of the first fragile green wave breaking on the shore.

The first wave leaves behind a tiny arc shape like a shell; the body of a sleeping woman, a cold trace of pale blue. The next wave reclaims her for the sea.

. . .

You shiver. 'It's cold, I must go.' Cold and dark. I'll come out with you, I've got to chop some more wood to stock up the stove for the night.

'Wait a minute,' slips in a young male voice like an eager tongue through the dark. 'Did I hear you say the sea is green?'

I did.

'Ha, the sea is never green, it is blue,' hisses the voice. Mr Jones spears the green sea words with a gleeful jab of his pen and hurries off, triumphant, to a draughty palace lodged in the darkness amongst the clouds. All of a fluster, all of a flurry, he sprints down corridor after corridor until, all of a sudden, he arrives breathless in an inner chamber, huge and sombre. Here, Mr Jones composes himself and bows elaborately before Mr Smith-god who is presiding from the throne. The green sea words slide to the ground like dying fish from a skewer.

After solemn consideration of the words suffocating at his feet on the marble floor, Mr Smith-god speaks: 'You have done well,' he booms. Then, after a carefully measured pause, in which the pointed nose of the inferior Jones points, furiously grateful, up and down, he lowers his tone. 'But not well enough!' Mr Jones scuttles into a corner.

'Out, snivelling fool!' booms Mr Smith-god, with such vigour that the walls of the palace shake and he has to hold his mouth closed tight to prevent the sickly pink sludge of slobbered pleasure which has accumulated there from oozing out and creating an indecent mess on the floor. At length, his mouth under control again, he continues, 'Go now and find me more. I want more! If you fail in this, you will be hung from a tower by your teeth. An ox will pull you by your tongue to a place where ants will nibble their way into your brain through your ears. Your eyes will be stuck with the pins of precious porcupines. Your nose . . .'

But I don't think I'll bother to waste any more of your time on this speech, because it does get very tedious after a while. Indeed, many hours before his master has finished, even Mr Jones has retired to his bedsit, the green sea words having quietly expired and died.

With Jane

Early in the morning they get off the bus. Early in the morning the cleaning women chatter as they scurry in a huddled group up the long drive to the hospital, like a bundle of busy leaves propelled by the wind. Looking up, they see a women is watching them from the window of the dayroom in the psychiatric wing.

'What did you say her name was?' remarks one to another.

'Who?'

'The one up there, by the window.'

'That's Jane. You know, the attempted suicide, came in last week.'

'Pills or wrists?'

They pause to score mud from their boots on the scraper by the steps.

'Pills, I think.'

'Four days,' thinks Jane.

For four whole days she has sat in her dressing-gown in the easy chair in the empty dayroom, staring out of the window at the cold lawn and the gravel drive which winds around it. Leaving the dayroom at mealtimes makes little difference, except that the chairs in the canteen are harder, the light brighter and there is a lot of noise. She sits in the canteen and there is the cold lawn on the plate before her, with gravy winding round it. She does not eat. She hurries back to the dayroom to the window. It is as if her life has been simply plunged underwater, but here there is no pain.

'Funny, how there's always one like that,' says one of the cleaning women to her friend later, as they vacuum down the corridor, away from the dayroom. 'There's always one that doesn't speak, sitting in that chair by the window.'

'Shame,' responds the other, 'pretty girl, they usually are, mind you . . .'

'Boyfriend trouble, I suppose.'

'Screamed the place down when she came in, you should have heard her!'

'They always do, then they are quiet.'

'Shame . . .'

The grey-green lawn wavers slightly under the opaque sheet of air on the other side of the window. Jane sees her shadow flicker sadly at the edge of the lawn beside a bare tree. She snatches it back to herself, as if it were a flimsy treasure and she a crab in an underwater cave.

On the fifth day, in the corridor, one of the cleaning women observes to the other that she has noticed the girl at the window was smiling as she looked out.

'Bad sign,' says the other, prodding the button for the lift. They are going to 'do' the next floor.

'I don't know why they look at me in that way, so full of pity,' whispers Jane, spitting out her smile on to the floor. 'No reason, not now. I like it underwater . . . sitting, watching the underwater life: a fish glances and a lobster stares . . . I sing to myself, secretly, softly in the depths and touching no longer hurts . . .' But in the next breath, she is mouthing his name, and he has left her . . . his name, her name, his name . . .

The black branches of the tree, standing with its shadow on the cold lawn, cease to waver like seaweed and become firm. Brave and black against the white air, stiller than still, stiller than staring . . . and then there is a shift. A shift like the sudden tight flick of the joint of a wrist, and the branches strain up a fraction. And now the branches are waving and wavering again, waving a streamer of sunlight back and forth, loosely and blithely.

Jane bends her head forward and presses her hand to the glass. Again she sees the branches strain up, expanding an opening in the sky and bowing gracefully towards her, brushing dapples of sunlight across the lawn as if they were sprinkling an offering of enchantment. So that she, like a tentative crab at the bottom of the ocean, is tempted to extend a trembling feeler out of her cave, then legs and body and . . .

'I push up into a tunnel of sunlight which filters down through the water. Arms straight up, legs kicking in the flickering. Heaving my way through the mass of tiny objects here suspended, I move through. Sea voyager, sky voyager, silent voyage through empty floating motion. I disrupt the pattern, sending crystal triangles spinning off against sea stars and hexagons, journey through a kaleidoscope. I move up.' She is rocking her body in the chair, but when she stops she sees the outside world is advancing grimly towards her, as if from above . . . the tree, with arms outspread, the lawn, the skin of the sea, they are all rushing towards her, swaying grotesquely . . . and there is nothing to stop them, nothing to hold on to in her flimsy underwater world. She clasps her hands to her head, waiting for impact, waiting for pain.

And now it comes, the drenching bewilderment, the sickness and then the pain and she remembers the reason for her being here and she remembers that he has left her and again she is mouthing his name. It is as if she had broken through the surface of the sea, that she were afloat on the open sea, but, looking out of the window, she sees that this is not so, for there is the still lawn, the bare tree and the stark fact . . . he has left her. And she is here, in a corner of the forlorn dayroom with its hideous furniture, afraid and lonely, crying quietly, fingering the corner of a handkerchief, muttering. Love? Life without him? . . . No life beyond, muttering his name, why?

'Because I am unworthy,' she tells herself, wrenching and twisting the material of the handkerchief, 'of course I am unworthy, my fault, yes, all my fault.' Now she must strike herself, she must beat and punish . . . for she is unworthy, wanting only this now: wanting to die.

In the corridor someone is laughing. Jane grits her teeth, clenches her fists and hits and hits her head with her knuckles, struggling to wipe herself out . . . not wanting people, not wanting light, struggling to sink. No one comes. The mocking laughter in the corridor ceases: there is quiet. She discovers that she is still afloat. Still afloat, the air is cold, ahead an empty, lonely land.

. . .

Towards evening, violet light intensifies across the plain. Jane, wrapped in her pale blue dressing-gown, lies on the flat yellow-tinged shore. She does not move. Her arms encircle her aching head. Her hair is lying on her arms. Her hair is brown. Her knees, under the dressing-gown, are pressed tight to her stomach. Sky darkens.

. . .

Another frozen February day, hard dry gift. When I wake on mornings like this I could cry with cold. The stove is difficult to light, but it's burning now. I sit quietly here in the boat, ready, I think, to untie the wrapping on the day; with the point of my blue pen I reach out to touch its frozen knot.

For a long time there is only silence . . . so I lean back in my chair against the wall, the thin edge of the room which divides me from the air and the water . . . and thoughts float out of the window and float with the ducks downstream on the river cold and smooth as glass.

'There are lots of worlds,' you say, suddenly, from the visitor's chair. My chair tips back into the room.

. . .

But, in a world which is dark, a woman on the beach moves her hand to her head. In the world which is dark, Jane strokes her own head. Her head hurts, there is still pain. Dark, silence and then day. She sits up slowly in the light. No sun, just a change of empty tone. She gathers her knees under her chin and looks out across the sea of grey and green.

. . .

Beside the Thames in London stands another institution, an art gallery. You and I are stepping through the hard grey streets. It's cold. We hurry up the stone steps, clutching our scarves; we could be characters in the opening scene of a film. It's Mr Jones who gives us the tickets to enter. 'Morning ladies,' he says, taking our money cheerfully.

34

We tread along the brightly lit corridor, explorers in a stone whale, and enter a chamber. A row of paintings on the wall this side, and a row of paintings on the wall that side; we look at this side first:

Picture one. The setting is ancient Egypt. The wide Nile winds slowly into the desert, where pyramids slice triangles in a round red sun. In the foreground a beautiful woman dangles her hand into the Nile.

Picture two. The working woman washing by the river glances up, her laughter freezes in oil paint.

Picture three. Foreground: stiffly swirling deep blue sea, and rocky cliffs on which stands a lonely straight tower. The navy sky behind is starry. At the top of the tower she waits alone, staring out of a contraption of headgear, patiently.

Picture four. Floating. Floating Pre-Raphaelite woman is borne through tangly undergrowth; her hand drags in the water which is littered with lilies.

Picture five. Softly, a punt divides the branches of the weeping willow; the river flows through Oxford in 1920. Again she sits, in the seat at the back of the boat, trailing her finger in the water.

Picture six. And so, transported into the present, she finds herself, inset, reclining beside a swimming pool in the heat. She sips a long, cool drink and stares.

Silence, silence which has been polished so that it hardens and shines like glass. I stand in front of picture six; she stares out, and I stare back unable to leave her, although I want to run away. Somehow I am stuck and so I stand, and we continue to regard each other in painful silence, stupidly, mutely . . . until I know that I do not believe this silence: this silence is a lie! Now I can move, I turn to you . . . but you are miles away along this endless row of pictures, gazing at a picture of your own.

'Come now, come this way, look over here.' The fat artist, Mr Smith-god, wears a clean smock; he has a paintbrush behind his ear. His hand is on my shoulder. With deceptive gentleness he steers me away from the silent women, and my cry is swallowed into the throat of the draughty corridor, and the age-old lie is bellowed back; it reverberates in the chamber. 'This is all!' More pressure is exerted on my shoulders. I am facing the other wall.

Horror. This wall is a teeming protraction of horror. It is seething and squirming with cruel activity. Here, with swords raised and flashing, crowds of men are clamouring. They force each other up the scaffold, into pots of boiling oil and out again. Digging their heels with pointed spurs into the flanks of terrified horses, they rear and claw and shoot away, trampling the sunset. So much noise my brain will burst: sirens shriek, horns blast, hot cries blister the air. Then, in its own time, the heavy rope from the gallows swings out long and slow, and shrugs the noise aside. I see a procession of elders slipping from the horizon of one picture into the next, where they assemble on a low dull hill and incline together in shrouded secret conference. Now, as one, the company promptly turns its snarling face, and wizened fingers steadily uncurl and dart out in furious accusing unison to point, identify, denounce, condemn . . . the condemned are the women who sit and stare silently through the squares of glass on the other side of the room. Mr Smith-god releases his hand from my shoulder; it is done.

I watch the women in the pictures; they are waiting. Silence. Something is waiting to blossom out of the moment when they dip their hands into the water. I know this silence is a lie, this silence will be cracked.

'Breathe into emptiness,' said the old woman, 'and what you breathe out is not emptiness, but flowering life across the plain.'

And now there are many of us here, sneaking in, casting glances over our shoulders to make sure Mr Smith-god is not looking. We set to work.

'For once there was breath between the painted layers.'

'For once there was our own full silence which hangs in the air like an expression of light around us.'

'And once there was a time when we did not fear pain.'

We prise the frames from the pictures of the women. We lift out the glass and send it smashing down the hall. Our fingers are bleeding. Red drops of blood and flakes of gold lacquer from the frames mingle on the floor. The women step down from the canvases, and now there is sound. The sound, the joyous stomp of our feet on the ground, as singing and laughter rises in a wave. The floor of the chamber flows green. Green tide floating out splinters of golden frame. The chamber divides; we have gone.

. . .

You and I stand on the stone steps outside the gallery, wrapping our scarves around our necks. It is cold, but the sky has lifted and is blue. 'I must go now,' you say.

I watch you climb the steps of the Hungerford footbridge to cross the river to Waterloo station. You reach the top and break into a run. Dodging in and out of the flow of people, cleverly, easily, you sing. There behind you, the row of pictures: men at war, at work . . . snuffling, chugging machinery; London. Buildings writhing their way up and tumbling down; when you cross the footbridge, you sing.

'How dare she? How dare she exalt!' booms a furious voice across the sky. For a while I scrutinise the skyline in vain, and then I spot him . . . Mr Smith-god, perched awkwardly on the dome of St Pauls. It is difficult to make him out; St Pauls is a rather insignificant nobble on the horizon nowadays, almost completely submerged by the vigorously thrusting edifices of its own acquisitive offspring.

'I dare, I dare, oh Mr Smith-god the now not-so-terrible!' With a brief wave you turn and become part of the crowd descending the steps on the other side.

. . .

The midday sun is streaming in through the window. I sit in my chair in the boat, tracing a doodle on my writing pad, and wistfully speculate. I speculate that I am following you on through a spiral of images: that when you step from the last stair of the bridge, the fragile thread of our connection does not break, but gently distends and that you are luring me after you; tossing your trail up in a loop like the thin wake of a salmon, you leap easily over the line on the page and thread your path down and away and away, until we are linked only by the suggested tremor of your tiny quick foot depressing faint curves along the strand of a spider's web to the edge of the writing pad, and my pen squiggles off the side of the page. You are gone. I am alone in the boat, and the day is open, and the gift is light.

. . .

Jane stands on the shingle of the pale shore, rubbing her shoulders to warm them. She watches as the sea strokes waves, green over green over green into the edge of silence which is vast.

'What's the point?' she thinks. 'What's the point in my being alive? Of course there are no answers to questions like these, no answers . . . just the empty, sickly slapping of water breaking on land, this nothing, nothing land which is hard, on which my feet stand for no reason whatsoever.' She stands and shivers, and the sound of the waves seems to merge into the silence, so that all around her there is complete and utter silence, which seems to travel like a conspiracy across the pale, unknown future of the land, across the endless, open ocean, reflecting distance from the sky . . . and with a crash the sound of the waves comes back. She pushes her hair away from her face, behind her ears.

'I'm glad I'm here.' She does not think before she speaks the words aloud. She is surprised she has said them so deliberately.

'But I have. Yes, it is me, Jane, who has spoken.'

After the words have been spoken, the silence retreats, and she watches wave after wave curl up with confidence into the hunched shape of question marks and break upon the shore.

'How far does it go, I wonder? How far and how deep does it go, this desolation of the sea?'

She bends down and, scooping a handful of water from the next wave, splashes it on to her face . . . cold. She stands up and turns away from the sea to the land. She cannot see very far; ahead of her is a shingle ridge which spreads like a wall along the length of the shore. At first, when she begins to climb, it is slowly. As her feet stick into the shingle, pebbles are dislodged and tumble down the bank and run splat, splat, splattering into the sea.

'When you can't think anymore the only thing to do is to go with the body,' she mutters to herself, climbing more and more quickly, pushing and scrambling up the slope . . . until she is standing at the top, panting.

38

The earth ahead rests silent and empty . . . like the sea, but very still. Dead or waiting? Jane catches her breath and reaches out her arms as if to smooth and steady the mirage-misty yellow plain, and there, in the distance, the crack stretches out under the sky close to the horizon. Beside the crack stands the tree, black branches upraised.

And then comes something creeping, a tiny black speck comes creeping along the top of the ridge towards her. Like a speck on the surface of a mirage, like a thought wandering out of a dream into consciousness, finding itself suddenly in the light . . . walks the cat.

The black cat reaches her and rubs against her legs. Jane bends down to greet her. 'Something else is living,' she says, stroking her back. The cat reaches up and nuzzles against Jane's cheek. The woman and the cat look up; the yellow wash of the morning is drying on the plain.

Then, all of a sudden, the cat plunges away down the shingle ridge. Jane follows. A trail of footprints and a trail of pawmarks lengthen across the waste behind them, towards the tree.

'It's strange,' says Jane, pausing a moment, 'in all this space I don't feel lonely, and as my feet touch the earth, at this particular point, and that, it's as if they fit into invisible footprints. As if there were already lots of little trails . . . invisible tracks, winding back and forth from the sea . . . it's sort of instinct . . . Maybe I'm just being silly,' she adds, hurrying on.

But, some yards ahead of her the cat stops. Her ears prick up, her head turns to one side. Into the silence lands an ugly black crash, a flash like the end of a fuse being lit. A dark blot of energy seeps into the corner of the landscape. Jane is surrounded by buzzing noise; she feels alone. The black blot pulses, larger and larger, at great speed towards them. The expanse of sky is shrinking; she is alone. Human arms and legs shoot out of the blot and retract, mechanical motion, mechanical noise. Now it seems to untwist into a chain of cardboard figures, black and white like newspaper cutouts, faces fixed, arms linked, legs kicking together. Kick to that side, kick to this side and step towards Jane. They kick over the traces in the sand, snatching steadily through the earth like a greedy caterpillar through a leaf. They chant in rhythm with their motion, jaws snapping.

'Snicker-snacker, snicker-snacker,
we are the women with too much to do,
jabbing at each other
in the supermarket queue.

A troop of go-go dancers,
paper dolls on a chain,
all of us in rhythm,
isn't it a shame?

You take the lead,
and we'll follow you
to work in the factory, to serve at the table,
to scrub out the bowl
in the public loo.

We raise our voices higher,
tie scarves under our chins.
We throw back our necks
and brightly twitter hymns.

Oh, we throw off colours,
we throw out words.
No time to ponder meaning,
the thought has not occurred.

See, our swallows are dead.
They fall to the earth . . .
But there's no time to look,
when you're strapped to the bench
and forced to give birth.

So, we cut across our pattern,
we snip through the curve,
we chew in the sky
to make a mince pie.

Snicker-snacker, snicker-snacker . . .'

The cleaning women unplug their vacuum-cleaners from the sockets in the far corner of the dayroom. Swiftly they coil the leads around the stomachs of the machines. The first machine is buffeted through the door and waits in the corridor, whilst its owner holds back the door so that her friend's machine and then her friend may glide through. The first cleaning woman closes the door very gently.

'She's talking to herself now,' she whispers.

'Shame. Such a pretty girl,' responds her friend, as they drag their machines down the hall.

Jane opens her eyes. There in the stillness is the yellow plain stretching away into the distance before her. At her feet a snarled black line is smouldering. Jane and the cat jump over the line and continue on their way towards the tree.

Now Ruby and Rebecca

Far out on the green sea sits a woman on a lily leaf, turning round and round, slowly.

Dark. Ruby stands in the rattling tube train, hanging on to one of those soft plastic things that dangle from the ceiling. Ruby seems to spend all her time in tubes, being dragged through her life, plunging forever from dark to light to dark, being tossed from side to side, being jostled, being pushed, being looked at. She knows that he is looking at her. She clings on to the dangling thing, dangling from the ceiling, very tightly as if she is frightened it will, at any moment, break off at the root, and she will be propelled out, over the shoulders of her fellow travellers, on to the steel lines below.

As she clings and sways, she occupies herself in catching her reflection in the window, now that he is concentrating on his crossword, now that he is no longer looking at her. Ruby has two reflections: one which flatters, one which distorts. She calls them, simply, her good and her bad.

Good reflection: blonde hair bouncing around a flat white-green oval face, pink lips, blue eyes blinking back at her underneath the poster advertising capsules to be taken to fight bad breath. The reflection wavers on the verge of a smile; it is smashed as the tube hurtles out of the dark into a bright station.

Bad reflection: the bad reflection arises in unwieldy fashion behind the sickly yellow grey fog in the smoker's carriage. Why the reflection is sometimes good and sometimes bad, she doesn't know. Perhaps this one is ill. It rises, a mottled pattern of shadows, swirling black under the eyes, around the mouth, and under the chin, so that the mouth and eyes are merely objects floating in black shadow holes. In the lost eyes in the bad reflection, there is a streak of wickedness. At one time, secretly, Ruby had found the bad reflection, which frightened her, the more fascinating of the two. Then she became her reflections: beautiful, ugly, light, dark . . . the train hurtling on, it didn't matter.

When she was younger, before she lost hope, she had worked for a while in the theatre. Under a single spotlight on the black stage, she sported her good reflection before the fat director and his thin friend who sat in the empty auditorium near the back, like the last two passengers on the late tube. She gained a small measure of success, they were gratified by her performance, her smile; the bounce of her blonde hair.

'We will give her a small part,' they agreed, out of "kindness".

But that was a long time ago. She had been forgotten. Now it seemed it had always been like this, herself being rocked inside the screaming train, herself on a floating lily leaf, way out on the deep sea, turning round and round, through day and night. The nights are longer now. She is older, but still attractive she supposes, for a woman in her late thirties. The colour in her hair, her lips, is fading in the stale air of the tube. When she stares at the reflections now they say nothing to her; the ugly is no longer more interesting than the attractive; the difference between them is fading too. She looks for her reflections even more urgently now, clinging to the habit. If the tube is very crowded, and she has to bend down to catch a glimpse of herself under the arm of the person standing next to her, so that her knees stick into the body of that person, and it is obvious what she is doing, well, she doesn't care. Mr Smith, sitting opposite, flaps open his paper and blocks the view.

So, Ruby is left behind, the sagging silhouette of a woman, bobbing away into the distance on a lily leaf over the green sea. When, from under the water, a whirling current grabs the leaf and spins her round to face us, then, sometimes, she will hoist a smile, a half wave, actress to her audience, queen to her people, but she turns away to face her own reflection and, self-absorbed, continues to comb her hair.

. . .

I step back, completely, into this particular February afternoon and look up from the page. The trees on the other side of the river

43

form a tiny black fringe at the edge of vast blank grey sky. But then, I think (and almost see for a second) won't it be incredible when those trees turn green! Lots of greens. I am so cold, they are so cold, that this thought welling up makes tears well up, as if nothing else matters except those trees which will turn green.

And I defy
The mute, cold sky,
And will be here to see,
The rebirth of the tree.

'Silly lady.' Mr Smith-god lowers his paper, is about to intervene, but the tube shrinks him away with Ruby into a dark tunnel.

. . .

With a screech of a whistle, the three-thirty train pulls out of Waterloo station. We sit behind one another in the long row of seats, so that all I can see of you is one brown-booted foot, sticking out into the corridor ahead of me. It is sunny. I am happy to be speeding out of London, on metal tracks bending smoothly across the surface of the living. I look out of the window and the world is fluid, a stream of windows and rooftops, thousands of tiny dots winking silver and red and black. Then I see her: Rebecca.

I see her in the shimmer of heat travelling over the rooftops. The vivid face and tortured figure of a woman caught in a towering thorn tree above the rippling roofs. Her eyes, wild, fighting eyes. Her hair long, bright and auburn, caught in the branches of the thorn tree. Thrashing. The train gathers speed; the more she thrashes in the tree, the more her hair becomes entangled with it. The thorns cut into her breasts as the branches stifle, then obscure her face.

Rebecca had planted the tree herself, a rose tree, to make her world beautiful. The thorns which dug so deeply into her flesh were the questions she asked about the world, the colour of the sky, about herself. The tools she had at her disposal, to tend the tree, were jagged and broken. The liquid she had bought in a little brown bottle to feed the tree, to help it grow, was poisoned. Her tree could not grow straight, for she had nothing with which to give it true expression. As the branches twisted and turned in on themselves, slowly she became furious inside. She spent more and more time with her tree. She transplanted it to a lonely place, she left her bed at night to slither towards it under the full moon. She wept alone in the dark.

By day she pretends to go around normally, tending to the household chores, tinkering with a painting in her studio room, doing the shopping . . . but people notice. She turns the corner in the supermarket, the gleaming gangway, lined with washing powder and pet food, has no end. The women leaning over wire trolleys have words buzzing round their heads. They part, suddenly, to let her through. Their eyes are following her, words like gnats swarming after her. 'Doesn't she look odd!' Out of the brightly lit supermarket into the dark streets. Rebecca cycles home to her tree.

Daily the obsession grows; her painting becomes the desperate attempt to give her tree beauty and a living form. She lies awake in her bed in the dark, and in her mind she is shaping branches, upwards, so that when the day comes the buds will see the light. She falls asleep and two men come with spades to dig up the tree; they plant it back upside down. Furiously, Rebecca tears her tree up and replants it, carefully washing mud from the few leaves that remain. She wakes; her tree cannot grow in this world. The sky is too heavy here. Even the sunny sky has the weight of Mr Smith-god's hammer pounding down through it.

As she lies thinking in the dark, and when she faces her canvas in the morning, Rebecca whispers questions to herself. 'Why am I doing this?' 'What am I trying to do?' 'What change am I trying to bring about?' . . . and she is met by laughter screaming through the supermarket, silence in the sky. Her questions become thorns, they thrive. Gently, the twisted branches tighten around her.

When I look up again only the eyes are moving. They are flashing wildly in the face of the woman whose body is caught in a burning bush. As we sway to a halt, out of the shimmering flat pond of seething activity which is London, the first heat of the year rises like an explosion into the sky.

There is a woman, far out at sea, turning.

There is a woman in the sky, burning . . .

But here is the train which stops at the station.

SECTION 5
Sun

February is almost over. Not that it makes much difference when you are enclosed underneath it; a cold damp day at the end of February is much the same as a cold damp day at the beginning of February.

You catch a glimpse of me in the mornings, opening my front door and quickly emptying the rainwater I have collected in an assortment of little pots and containers from the places where my roof leaks, into the river. Later the door opens again. I appear in a red anorak. Bravely I make a dash through the slanting rain, armed with my saw and my axe, to the woodpile in the corner of the yard. Hastily I chop some wood and retreat.

But, as the same frozen day creeps over me again and again, there is a change in the river. Each afternoon the river rises higher than the day before, lapping up into the boatyard, covering the gangplanks so that I am cut off. When the water retreats, it leaves behind a different arrangement of old cans, shoes and sticks on the concrete slipway.

It is afternoon. I am cut off. The rising river makes the boat jerk awkwardly from side to side, like an animal irritated by the rain. And . . . it's grey outside, and . . . I don't know where you are . . . and sometimes the open plain seems to exist far, far away, beyond reach. It would be so easy now to switch on the radio and drift off into the evening, washing my hair, reading. I look down at my cat, who is asleep sprawled out on the carpet in front of the stove; she stirs and smiles, before going back to sleep, without the pain of indecision.

. . .

Jane stands alone on the empty yellow space of the plain and the cat sits beside her like this full stop. Behind her, black smoke is dispersing slowly above the jagged trail left in the earth by the snicker-snacker women. Following the black line, in the distance, the soft undulation of the shore is touched into place by the green sea. Ahead of her the golden crack runs on, wet as a wound. The tree seems tiny, naked, tiny.

'I am too late,' she thinks, as her eyes confront the wall of blank mist towering beyond the tree. She moves to go, but there, behind her, is the black line smoking grimly. It is blocking her way.

'So this is it. A line of light and a line of dark, and I must spend my time like a shuttle, trailing backwards and forwards between them. It doesn't make sense.'

But when she turns again to face the line of gold, it seems that it has shifted up a little, like the frame of a loom, and quivering threads of light are beginning to spread out from the base of the tree, between the lines; over the crack, under the black tear, around the rim of the shore, over, under, and back, weaving firmly and gently binding.

I watch them walking towards the tree, the cat with her tail in the air. Jane holds her head down. I feel uneasy. She is a solitary figure whose face I cannot see, an unknown person, convenient symbol sent to mark a spot in the waste . . . my observation is inadequate, a feeble gesture; somehow it's like placing a stone over the body of the unknown soldier.

'But you are not wrong to mark the courage of the unknown woman.' You speak from a distance. I do not know where you are.

The woman walks on, clutching her pale blue dressing-gown around her neck, on through the emptiness of the land, in the direction of the light. Beside her the cat, as there is so often a cat with the woman alone, the cat at ease with the discoveries of isolation. They come to a halt.

'What does all this mean?' says Jane. The words run off freely, they leap and echo across the plain.

'What does it mean?' The words march back in the guise of another voice, as if they had adopted a uniform. Then, like a great hill emerging from the bare earth, and like an army rising above that hill, the very much enlarged face of Mr Smith-god comes billowing and prickling up over the horizon. He establishes his position by sinking the points of his elbows into the yellow earth.

'What does it mean?' he repeats the words sternly. As he continues to speak, the form of his face is puckering and swelling into different faces, which reinforce each other like the drab manoeuvres of an army on a bare hill.

'You will not find meaning out here, little girl. Oh no. You are very wrong to venture out here, without knowing why, without a meaning. This is madness. You must come back.

'Jane, this is why I took you in my arms and put you away in a safe place where, in time, I would have given your life a meaning. I would have given you the very thing you are searching for.

'You must not turn your back on me, Jane. I am gentle. I understood your madness and I forgave you, although that wasn't easy. Then I took you away, so that you would not destroy yourself, to protect you.

'For that is what you tried to do, wasn't it? You tried to destroy yourself by swallowing pills. That is a great sin. But I forgave you . . .'

(There is a pause in which the features in the face crawl together and strengthen as blankness intensifies into rage.)

'But what do I find now? After all my effort? . . . Just as I was beginning to think I might trust you again? Why, I discover you have slipped away and are to be found wandering out here, without purpose, in this madness, this terrible madness. You had better come back, Jane. Come back here at once!'

Jane tries to distinguish the different faces: her father? the doctor? the vicar? as they merge into one another in the sky. She cannot scream, she cannot cry out. Slowly she becomes aware that, although the faces are transitory, the voice which issues from them is consistent, running towards her like a mercenary soldier, head ducking, concentrating on its purpose. Closer now, it creeps over the ground on its belly and, shielding itself with the mask of a 'lover', it whispers in her ear: 'You are mad Jane, you are without meaning.'

Now it is inside her, inside her stomach. It swells up into an inflated head of fear, carefully crushing her spirit with its pressure,

48

suffocating her systematically from inside. It subsides, draining out of her in a twist of pain, and she is lying face down on the earth, her knees gathered to her stomach, her arms across her head, protecting her newly bruised and splintered soul against the waste. The persecutor looks down at her and, as if prompted by an afterthought, ties her ankles and then her wrists together, and leaves. And the face in the sky becomes the curl of a hook, hanging in readiness to drag the woman away, in the name of the father and of the son . . . I feel sick.

· · ·

In the waiting moment, Jane slides a glance under her arm across the plain, away from Mr Smith-god. She is answered directly by a flicker on the horizon. The flicker is followed by a transfusion of colour which blazes boldly orange into the skin of the sky and becomes a tree. She sees an angry woman's shape grow and struggle in the centre of the tree. The surrounding sky drips new bright blue.

Rebecca, struggling in her thorn tree, struggles free with a yelp like a wild woman bursting out of the undergrowth and, battered and bleeding, comes charging across the plain. Shaking her fist at the grey male manifestation above, she cries out:

'Beware, beware
Mr Smith-god, beware
for I am angry.
And in my anger
I shall tear
the fleece of your face
down from the sky.
That you should dare
to hurt my sister,
to isolate her
in a dreary waste,
between your frozen gulfs
of "meaning".'

'Huh,' sniffs Mr Smith-god, 'she is hysterical.' But as he mutters on, his words become blurred and then inaudible, as if the soldiers have deserted the blank hill. After taking stock of the situation, his grey face begins to wilt until it has vanished, gone, leaving only a feeble smear in the air, waiting to be erased by the vivid blue reaching up from the other side of the plain.

Now in a flurry of red and green clothing, now like a woman learning to fly, Rebecca storms across the waste, grasping the corners of the new blue sky, and holds it up, like an infinite cloak above her head. The cloak unfurls at great speed and lifts up and out over the plain, miles and miles of blue silk sky, shimmering. As the new blue spreads up, the film of paleness which preceded it recedes at the far end of the earth.

Jane wriggles her wrists and, finding the end of a cord between her fingers, unravels the fastening which secures them. She props up her head on her arm.

'We have had enough of grey,' she remarks to the cat, as they watch the new blue lift and lift above them. Silence . . . then her little remark gathers an echo:

From place to place
and over and under,
defying grey distance.
Though we read and write
or we wash and we clean;
yet, we weave and we spin,
and our song is a song of colour
rising in the earth.

Beside the rocking loom, at the heart of the song, the old woman pauses to sort her threads, then, one by one, she works them deftly into the fabric of the plain, and a band of leaf green hope grows next to the golden crack, and the pale yellow earth waxes strong yellow, shot with varying shades of red, the many shades from ages of suffering spilled into the living cloth.

Rebecca lets go of the corners of the blue cloak, leaving it to float alone above, and stands, hands on hips, at the far end of the plain, staring at the spot where Mr Smith-god disappeared. (He is lost down below somewhere, desperately trying to order the dead skins of the sky which collapse and collapse like empty parachutes on top of him.)

And Jane . . . a tiny but definite line, lying on her back on the

50

plain, conscious of the immensity of the blue sky above her, threads her own, new vision into the spirit of the song. She threads her vision with tenderness, perceiving that all the colour in this vast space is also contained in the smallest, most fragile of feelings which flicker open minute by minute in the palm of the hand like butterflies blushing their bright wings in the light.

. . .

The bands of colour in the fabric are now spun taut; firm enough for the old woman to take the square of material from her loom and smooth it out like the fragment of a map on her knees. Jane stands up. Around her the softest fingers of light are moving about on the plain, highlighting the colour with their touch, gold and green and yellow and red, and over and over again on their colourful journeys, the shafts of light meet and combine for a twinkling instant, as do the crosscurrents of water on a calm sea. Flat, bright stillness rises in her breast, laying down her shape in shadow beside her. There, in the distance, is Rebecca.

Rebecca is looking towards a point on the horizon where her bush of energy is opening, flowering in flame. Then, as she watches, the bush loops inward into a perfect orange sphere. The sphere intensifies like an eye, and the eye winks out the first ray of solid sunlight across the plain. Rebecca leaps off along the blazing yellow trail towards the new sun, as when we are young we charge at the sun. Twigs from the thorn tree, still tangled in her hair, fly from her, alive now with the burning energy of the sun ray, so that she is a blazing figure running forward under the blue sky. Reaching the far end of the plain where the sun has risen, she grows tall, and stretching up her hand plucks the sun down out of the sky; it struggles, them comes to rest in her arms. Jane is amazed.

And, slowly, balancing the sun on her arm, Rebecca leans the length of her body back, so that her red hair touches the earth behind her. The sun rolls down her arm and collects in a ball in her hand. She draws her arm back, and her hand, rising like a wheel beside her body, releases the ball of light into the sky. The sun goes hurtling through the blue at great speed, showering the earth with gold on gold.

The world begins to spin. Jane is running, is running hard, thrusting her feet down over the waving bands of colour, knowing that if she stops she will fall, knowing that she will not stop, she will not fall. And the plain, the tree, the cat, begin to revolve around her, slowly at first, like satellites. She is striding smoothly, faster and faster, until in slow motion she reaches up her arms . . . and 'plop' she has caught the sun in her hands, like sun in a cup.

'Over here!' shouts Rebecca, standing on the green verge beside the crack. She watches Jane, a tiny figure in the distance, lift the ball of light, then hurl it back up into the blue again, towards her. But it flies past and is rapidly swallowed into the mist on the other side. The new colour of the plain slackens and begins to lose its vibrance, shrinking away after the sun . . . then appears to change its mind, quickening once more as the flaming ball re-emerges from the mist and bounces down at her feet. Rebecca catches it and throws it straight up into the sky, where it finds a space and remains.

And the cat? For a long time the cat crouches, absorbed by a tiny drop of light which has fallen from the main sphere to the earth. She gives it a pat with her black paw; and now she is dribbling it across the plain to the crack, where, with a concentrated swipe, she putts it into the golden liquid. Jane, Rebecca and the cat watch the speck of light bob away towards the sea. When it has vanished, they turn and walk towards each other in the sunshine.

. . .

'Dear me, it looks bad,' says Mr Smith-god to Mr Jones, as their highly polished shoes strike the highly polished floor in a drab corridor painted off-white, off-yellow or off-blue (it doesn't really matter). He lays a paternal arm across the shoulder of his inferior, and they pace off together, mumbling gravely, shaking their heads and nodding to one another. Both are wearing white coats, stethoscopes like loose human organs sticking oddly out of their pockets.

SECTION 6
Serpents and Ferns

It's ten to six in the evening – not yet dark. The water hasn't crept quite so high into the yard today. The light is shrinking away across the river, drawing silk into a vacuum. The angles of the battered objects in the yard protrude into the air. The trees stand firm. I slide the curtains across the diminishing light, one by one, shutting it out deliberately. I pause, face framed by the window, to watch two ducks paddling by in my little backwater in exactly the same way as when I watched them two hours ago; paddling through the reflections of the ivy and the cars drooping down from the car park, then back down the wide river . . . they are building a nest beneath the bridge. I shut them out.

Inside, I drop another log into the stove and sit down.

Being out on the plain with Rebecca and Jane has made me glad to retreat inside here, in my own little world; it's made me want to think about houses, nests, dry-smelling places where people collect objects. I could spin a life around these objects, arranging them, cleaning them, mending them. Most of the objects in here are old. Well, oldish and worn, made for different reasons by different people in different places: a bamboo table, an iron stove, an impressionist print. And I'm wondering about the individual quality of each, with its unknown history, gathered here in an arrangement of hard and soft, rounded and square shapes and lines . . . I'm looking at the difference in the way the light from the stove reacts on the surface of the mirror, the ceiling, the texture of the oil painting.

There is a vase of daffodils standing on the record player; I have put some sticky buds in with them. The old ones, the daffodils I threw away yesterday, had opened out into a collective yellow glow before they died, but these are new, single little bells of light tipped down amongst the sticky buds, pointing up.

And so, this evening, I don't know precisely what I am trying to say, what particular point I am trying to establish . . . just rambling contentedly around the room . . . across the page, wondering, woolgathering, thought gathering; as if each object held a fruit which could be plucked and stored. And I'm wondering about different lives in different places and wondering especially about you reading this and I hope you are not bored . . . and I wonder if it *is* possible to spin a thread from this boat on the river out to you . . . but I haven't the energy for that now . . . so, putting down my writing pad, I pick up the book I'm reading and lean back in my chair, into another world.

. . .

Morning. A brave and beautiful morning and I begin a new sheet. There is actually sun on the trees across the water; not bright, brilliant sunshine, but a soft spring sunlight, so that the trunks and branches of the trees are not black any longer . . . they are greenish brown. The river is calm. A single ray of sun is spreading into the houseboat from the corner of the window and my plants seem to be stretching out towards the day with more effort than usual.

'It won't last long,' says Mr Smith-god, pinning a cardboard cloud, with slanting black lines streaking out of it, on to a map of the British Isles; importantly delivering the weather forecast.

. . .

Morning, in another place. Unlocking the door of her room in the university residence, Helen is confronted by the squat oblong of her newly made bed. The moss green bedcover is tucked down tightly; above the bulge of the pillow rests a wreath of faint perfume . . . the cleaners have been in already and made the bed whilst she has been at breakfast. She flings herself down on to the bed and fumbles for a cigarette. Stunned after the struggle of getting to the dining-room and back, dragging behind her the unwieldy shadow of a dream through a network of corridors, she lies on her bed like one in an arena; having fallen off her chariot of dreams, she watches the horses without their charioteer speed away from her, towing her little cart out of the window and across the new morning sky. New morning and she has been dropped in the same place to be absorbed into the crowd in the lecture theatre . . . but not yet.

So, she lies, listening to the gurgling of the water spreading round the pipes from radiator to radiator . . . so, she lies, a little tense, wondering if the woman next door, who is in the third year, is going to put a record on. No. With relief, Helen hears the sound of a key being turned in a lock from outside in the corridor . . . footsteps retreating. The woman must be leaving for a lecture. Now, if only she can forget the water charging around in the radiators, she will be free. Water in iron pipes; not hot water, lukewarm water.

She leans over to the bedside table and picks up this book. Good morning Helen, she reads.What do you feel when you pick up this book, I wonder? Is it all right? I mean, you're not bored, are you? Helen turns and slowly stubs out her cigarette, self-conscious, aware of being observed. She mutters something to herself.

'No, I'm not bored,' she replies politely. 'I don't know, I feel different things . . . depending on the distance between us, that is. In the beginning, when I came creeping up to you in the boatyard, I felt sort of meek like a child. I found you, and you seemed to be like another child on the edge of a vast shore, creating a world for herself in a rockpool. You invited me to play with you, and we looked, whispering, into the pool. When I got tired, I just went away, back to my own pool on the beach, but carrying some of your water in a bucket.'

She sits up.

'But this is different, because now you have come creeping over to me. You are peering through my window and you want me to come back, I suppose, to your pool. But I'm not sure if you really want to play . . . or if you do, it's on your terms, for your purpose . . . you want me to become a character in your book.'

I'm sorry. All this dodging about, backwards and forwards, is because I feel that I have something I want to protect. It's risky; I'm torn between the need to share it with you, and the feeling that at all costs the most important thing to do is to preserve, protect. Which is silly, because it is already shared knowledge anyway. I'm scared that you might disturb my pool and call me unrealistic, mad. On the other hand, I know you have your own pool and I must respect that there are things you might do or think that you might not wish me to see or . . .

'You could always just push me into your pool you know, and hold me under! In a way I wish you would . . . pools? Honestly! . . . *Pools*? . . . Sorry,' she adds, 'but, that's the trouble . . . all this "sorry" business turns into a game of blindwoman's buff, in which we stumble about saying "sorry" to one another in the dark, or a polite form of hide-and-seek; it gets exaggerated, all this valuing of each other, so in the end you don't feel you have the right to write and I don't think I have the right to contradict! Yet . . . I suppose we are on the same beach at the edge of the plain, carrying little bucketfuls of twinkling secrets over to each other.'

Helen, on the beach, turns away and walks back to her own story, water dripping from her bucket. I follow her in order to describe.

. . .

So, lying on her bed, somewhere in the depths of the university complex, Helen lights another cigarette. There is only half an hour of peace left because she has a lecture at eleven. The lecture is to be on D. H. Lawrence; for this lecture, she is supposed to read some poems:

> 'I love you rotten,
> Delicious rottenness.'

It is all so boring! Lawrence himself, being the virile type, would have found it tedious being sectioned off like this, worker bees in the concrete hive of the university. Bees serving what? or whom? . . . 'No, here we have less sense than bees,' thinks Helen.

She has no idea what is behind it all, what this power might be, hiding, veiled and remote in a concrete chamber under the university, emanating sombre, electric blue and violet gloom. Perhaps the pumping power which people submit themselves to in this place is the same power which is shoving the water through the iron pipes from radiator to radiator. The trouble, she is sure, is that nobody has the faintest notion what it is they are supposed to be serving; the higher up in the hierarchy they are, the less they know, and so it becomes more and more important for them to pretend. Thus, she has noticed that the lecturer bees buzz more frantically than the student bees, as they tear round the corridors, flashing empty ideas at each other from piercing, frightened eyes. When the bends in the corridors are narrow or their paths become congested at the foot of the stairs, they engage in empty insect combat, mounting each other in an awkward flurry of insect feelers and terrified eyes. In the pockets of battle, the volume of the general battle, now greatly increased, is cut through every now and again, by the sound of a lash, as bees grow tails like scorpions in order to whip the fine thread of a sting into the enemy's flesh.

'I do not love you, rottenness,' says Helen, 'you are not delicious, you are neither sweet nor savoury, you are dead. Bits of dead matter, being pieced together into a hollow structure, ready for Mr Smith-god or D. H. Lawrence to kick back into the soil of England! . . . There is nothing wrong, I suppose, in reading Lawrence, if you want to read Lawrence, but if you don't, why bother?'

She stubs out her cigarette into the pottery ashtray she has brought from home, picks up this book again and reads . . .

. . .

In this new morning on the boat, for the first time this year, I go to open my little window. I have to force it, as if I were pushing a door open from inside a snowdrift. Now, for a moment, I catch a glimpse of the plain. In the distance I see Jane, Rebecca and the cat, standing on the green beside the crack.

'What sort of green do you mean? light green? dark green? village green?' snaps the voice of Mr Smith-god, as if with a question he could force my vision back.

But I can hear other voices, the voices of two women talking beside the crack.

'This landscape is rather flat,' says Rebecca.

'Well, we are not in the Bible,' says Jane , 'we can't just ask for a hill and there is one!'

'Bloody good job we are not!' replies Rebecca. 'You know what would be happening in a minute if we were . . . a slithery, slimy serpent would be slithering slimily towards us . . . to *tempt* us!'

'Anyway,' says Jane, 'we've got one already . . . we have got a golden, liquid serpent gliding along in the crack.'

'Right,' says Rebecca, 'and I don't think serpents are bad anyway, in fact . . .'

The words are strong and clear. However, others might not agree; they might perceive this conversation very differently, as does, for instance, Mr Jones, who happens to overhear it whilst standing at the bus-stop on his way to work. Mr Jones perceives it as an example of the idiotic nonsense women talk, when they have been inadvertently let out (together!) to have breakfast in a café . . . they should be at home cooking bacon and eggs for their husbands or doing the vacuuming. So, plucking an arrow from the secret pocket in the lining of his raincoat, he takes aim at one of the offensive women, sitting laughing in the café. But . . .

'In fact . . . I like golden serpents!' a female voice prances from the table in the corner of the café clean out of the window and lands on the pavement with spectacular agility.

'In fact, I especially like golden serpents, glorious, golden, glistening female serpents!' yells Rebecca, across the distance of the plain.

Luckily, as the glass in the windows of the sedate café shakes to the point at which it is in danger of splitting with the sound of women's laughter, the number 81 bus comes lolloping faithfully around the bend in the road beside the tobacconist's. Mr Jones is borne away to safety.

And here we go again, rollicking out across the plain . . . except I haven't got the energy now. Besides, Helen must put down this book and go to her lecture, and I have got to go and sign for my money at the social security.

. . .

Later . . . it's six-thirty p.m. Although I shut the window long ago and I've lit the stove, I've only just closed the curtains.

'Ahem.' Mr Smith-god assumes the authority of a schoolmaster, peering over my shoulder to survey the page on my desk. 'I asked you what sort of green. More precisely, what is it that is green beside the crack?'

Actually, I haven't got a desk yet, so I write this on to scrappy bits of foolscap paper balanced on my knee. Virginia Woolf had a special sort of paper to write on which she got from the Omega Press; Stevie Smith had yellow paper. Another little detail; I have a large wastepaper basket beside me, into which I occasionally toss the wrappers from my tobacco, but never any of these hard-wrought words. Colette said that her wastepaper basket was always overflowing with discarded words. Perhaps when I get a desk and set the wastepaper basket in place beside it, it will overflow as well, like a potted plant.

'You digress,' reproaches the voice, breathing closely down my neck. A fat hand is splayed out on the surface of my imaginary desk . . .

'What sort of green? What is green?'

Well, Mr Smith-god . . . I spin round like a cat and, looking straight into his flabby face, which is puckered all over with paternal benevolence of the most vile and simpering sort, I hiss . . . Ferns! Bright green ferns! . . . lovely, willowy, fronded ferns!

He is taken aback: or, to be more precise, he is physically thrown against the wall by my words. He recovers his composure and, extending a fat arm, proceeds to pat me on the shoulder.

'Alright dear,' he says, gathering his face together in preparation to relaunch himself down another slippery slope of condescension. I shudder beneath his patting; it makes me feel sick, like when you have to shake hands with the vicar.

Ferns! I hiss. All of a sudden he has melted away.

Well, it doesn't seem as if I am going to be able to do it now; to bring back the calm of the ferns and the crack. It's just words now, but they seem incredibly funny and powerful at the moment . . . fancy being able to send Smith and Jones running with a simple cry of 'serpents' or 'ferns'!

SECTION 7

Eggs

In the afternoon of the following day, I sit down, annoyed with myself for my late start, annoyed with myself for being so frivolous in what I wrote yesterday. I awoke suddenly this morning, having passed through a vast, shadowy cathedral dream and out through the softly coloured light of a stained-glass window image of the plain at the far end . . . through colour, back into consciousness.

Those colours have been with me all day, and now, in the late afternoon, I can see them clearly, firmly imaged as stained glass. The golden crack slips away around a corner, tucked into the vibrant green ferns; such fullness and depth as, I should imagine, rests on the land after a tropical storm. But these are colours I have never known to exist in any landscape I have visited before, they are so bright: anemone colours, stained-glass window colours, laid flat against each other, fleeing away into the distance.

Rebecca and Jane are resting amongst the ferns, lying on their stomachs, feet in the air. Their heads are hanging over the bank at the edge of the crack. The golden liquid flows beneath them, just out of reach on its journey from the west to the east, towards them, under them and away. They lie in silence, preoccupied with the sparkling patterns on the surface, introducing their own thoughts into the patterns, like dancers on to a dance floor. But the liquid, running swiftly, has no time to form static individual reflections; instead, it shines light up into their faces, golden light, as if an endless field of buttercups were being floated under their chins . . . to see if they liked butter.

Jane looks up to see the sun's fall from the sky. The branches of the tree cradle it, then let it slip, spinning down the straight black trunk.

60

. . .

Helen steps out, at last, on to the concrete steps in front of the literature department; the afternoon seminar has been particularly tedious.

At the same time, at the other end of the sprawling campus, the cleaning women, who have snicker-snackered their way through the day, are emerging in a line from an obscure door at the foot of the block of student residences. Elsie is the last to come out. As she stands buttoning up her coat, she pauses, taking notice of the red glow of the wintry sun spinning into the tops of the trees behind the library.

The line of women, wearing raincoats of various pastel shades, fades like a rainbow along the path in the direction of the supermarket. The two at the back stop and turn round.

'Come on, Elsie!'

'No, it's all right, Mary, I don't need any shopping today,' Elsie shouts back. And, doing up the last button on her pale green raincoat, she realises how pleased she is at the prospect of going home alone, even though it would have to be eggs again for tea.

'I think I'll walk home this evening instead of catching the bus, seeing as it has turned warmer . . . through the park,' she says to herself.

. . .

Jane rolls over on to her back. She shivers, tiny, alone. The emptying sky has a beckoning quality, enticing her back to the edge, to the barren shore; silence. She curls over towards Rebecca.

'You all right?' says Rebecca.

'Yes.'

As they lie there quietly, there is a rustle in the vegetation a little way off; the cat slowly uncoils herself from her nest in the ferns and stretches. Then, tail in the air, she trots through the undergrowth and, settling herself down beside Jane, goes back to sleep.

In the flickering darkness which is now closing in over the plain, a low sound like a chant begins to rise from the foot of the tree where the old woman sits in the shadows, spinning her evening song into the air. The thread of her song spreads out, loose and easy, fluctuating in an invisible spiral, now near, now far. Gently, Rebecca and Jane are drawn into this strange oscillating movement of sound as fragments from the old world are composed into a new time.

In the second before sleep, Rebecca looks across the crack and nudges Jane. Behind the dark mist screen on the other side, they catch a glimpse of two women walking . . . separately, one behind the other. They walk on, then seem to evaporate into the mist as if they had not been there at all.

. . .

Helen has decided against going to the coffee bar – it would be too depressing, especially at the end of the day. Neither does she want to go back to her room. At this time the residences would be buzzing with activity: people preparing meals in the communal kitchens, busily occupied with the business of pretending to look after themselves. This activity was merely a charade on independence; in fact, the students tended to become more and more alike every day, eating the same food (canned soup and spaghetti bolognese) bought in the same place . . . the supermarket on the campus. So she would go to the park, where she would have some peace.

Exhilarated by the idea of having some time alone, conscious of her capacity to detach herself, if only slightly, from the rest, she flees down the concrete steps and out under the arts block where the motorbikes are kept. As she is running up the hill, impatient now to get to the park before the sun has set completely, she sees one of her lecturers walking down the path towards her, carrying a briefcase bulging with essays.

The lecturer is of the thin, wiry, Mr Jones variety, lonely, always hungry for companionship, but unable to communicate. The important thing is to avoid his attaching himself to her. His means of doing this never varied: he would allude to his loneliness to make you feel sorry for him and thus coerce you into going for a 'quick' drink with him. But, once seated in the bar on the university campus, always the same seat, the unwary sympathiser would rapidly be impaled against the wall, like a reluctant snail being pecked at by a sleek, male bird. He would then begin to peck and peck at you in order to extract from you points about your existence which would confirm his own. At the end of it all, you felt empty and exhausted.

'It's a pleasant evening,' he chirps, quickly setting down his briefcase and carefully adjusting his little checked scarf, which does not need adjusting, into his beige coat.

'Yes,' says Helen, unenthusiastically.

Silence.

'Ahem,' he clears his throat. She shouldn't have given him that space; clearing their throats always gives them the upper hand. Silence again; she grabs the initiative . . . 'I'm sorry, I'm going to visit someone.'

It sounds very weak, but before he has time to ask her: Where is she going? Does she really have to go? Isn't his need, perhaps, greater? Or perhaps he could come too? Or at least walk with her part of the way? A walk would do him good, he has been teaching all day and . . .

'Goodbye,' she says, 'see you on Thursday,' and makes a dash for the shadows in the park.

The lecturer picks up his briefcase slowly . . . then, to prove to himself that he is really not much affected by the incident, and, of course, he has been well-trained not to be too much affected by anything, he assumes a bright smile and hops off down the path in search of further prey.

. . .

'At last! How reassuring it is, to step out onto the grass . . . like descending from an enormous air-machine on to the earth again,' says Helen.

(There has been a bit of fidgeting at the gate between Helen and myself over who would get into the park first and continue the narrative.

'Why are you so reluctant to hand over to me?'

I don't know. I don't want to be left out, I suppose.

'Oh, come on! Do I, your faithful reader, have to tear the story from you to make it my own?'

63

OK, I say, left behind at the gate . . . you carry on, but make sure you do a good job. Not too many adjectives! I shout . . . I stammer, as Helen runs off across the grass and into the trees with the narrative tucked under her arm.)

'. . . and smaller and smaller and smaller and smaller,' she sings. 'The park is becoming smaller, microscopic . . . "tinier than the hip bone of a termite"; I read that in an old spell . . . and it's all wrapped up like a spider's egg, hidden in the grass at the foot of the ugly air-machine. That's why I come here in the evenings; it's safe. I can get my jeans muddy and breathe.

'My bag isn't heavy. I can feel the shapes of the books inside it. Carry them away, carry them away from the ugly air-machine. Now they are mine again, they are comforting and they need comforting in a strange way, too . . . like baby birds with their mouths open, waiting for concentration to be poured into them.

'Along the path, under the trees to the river. The river was diverted when they built the university. Somehow, they must have hitched it up on prongs of their machinery and dumped it into raw channels they dug into the ground. Just like everything else . . . they allow the river to run on, but they control it . . . like a wild animal, brought in a crate to the zoo, is released and allowed to run the length of her cage. Running and running.

'And when, earlier this afternoon, I gazed out at these trees from the top of the arts block, where I sat in a hollow room which was ringing like a bell with empty words summoning the faithful to prayer, I felt that the real prayer was out here. Out and beyond, falling with the sun in between the dark speckled treetops, permeating the surface of a transparent wintry spider's egg . . . and so it is. The sun has gone and I am under the shell, where little pools of sacred shadow collect and cling. Safe. I choose this tree and place my bag of books at its roots. It's still warm enough to sit for a while and smoke a cigarette . . . and listen to the silver river, running earnestly along the length of her cage.'

. . .

'Eggs,' thinks Elsie, 'yes, eggs and bacon . . . and there's that tin of tomatoes in the fridge.' The click of the park gate cuts through

64

these snicker-snacker thoughts, and they fall from her like a chain. 'It's nice to have some quiet, after being with those vacuum cleaners all day.'

The chiffon scarf, tied under her chin, is scratching her; she takes it off, stuffing it into her empty shopping bag, and allows the evening air to fill her thoughts with romance. 'This must be where the students come to do their courting,' she says.

But, somehow, her thoughts don't take a grip on her as usual, although they come drifting across the grass and circle round her body buttoned up in her raincoat, this evening she seems to be able to control them, like the plastic hula hoops she twirled round her waist as a child; when she stops twirling, they fall to the ground, jingle, jangle, the red, the green, the yellow, and she can step out and wander off to do something else. So the evening simply carries her along further into itself, and she feels secure, as if soft garments were unfolding around her.

'Unfolding . . . that's it, unfolding like the sea.'

Unfolding as she used to years ago, making love to her husband when they were young, unfolding at the end of the day into the tiny flat where they lived when they were first married . . . before that, unfolding to a lover in a park like this, behind the trees in the dark . . . and a long, long time ago, unfolding towards her mother. This earliest unfolding had been, perhaps, the most complete unfolding of all. When she was a child, awakened by a bad dream in the middle of the night, she had cried out; her mother had appeared at the door and scooping her up, she was so tiny then, had carried her off to her own bed. Her mother smelt of perfume and setting lotion and little Elsie had unfolded into her arms. Her mother was dead now. She had died shortly before Elsie married.

'Strange that I should be thinking of her now . . . she hasn't crossed my mind for a long time.'

Elsie thinks of the nights when her own children cried out to her. Diane had gone through a period of wetting the bed when she first went to school.

'And come to think of it, didn't I do the same too?'

Night after night, her own daughter's cries had drawn her up out of a dream and floated her, quietly so as not to wake her husband, along the hall, her fingers claiming a clean nightie from the top of a pile of laundry in the airing cupboard as she tiptoed past. When she turned the handle on the door to the child's bedroom, the crying stopped. Sleepily, the shadowy form of the child raised itself on to its knees on the bed and held up its arms; Elsie peeled up the wet nightie and slid it off over the head of the little body, which shivered naked for a second in the dark. It would only be for a second. For Elsie had already rolled up the material of the dry nightie, ready to drop it over Diane's head as soon as the wet one was off. When it was on, she lifted the child up to sit on her hips, and they crept back along the hall, Elsie with one hand under her body and the other supporting the heavy head, holding Diane as she had held her when she was a baby.

Elsie had always taken Diane into her own bed, so as not to have to go to the trouble of changing the sheets in the middle of the night. Once in bed, Diane relaxed completely into sleep, curled up against her. But Elsie remembers that she herself had never found it easy to fall asleep again, as if the flood of dreams had retreated and left her like a stranded whale staring out over the sea in the dark.

'I wonder if my mother managed to sleep again when she took me into her bed?' she says out loud all of a sudden. 'Come to think of it, she did always seem very tired when I found myself in bed beside her in the morning.' A single bed, under the window; Elsie's mother was a widow. 'And . . . when I woke her up by cuddling in close . . . she looked a bit odd, a bit like a very old whale in the sea.'

'Someone is coming!' The thought that it might be her lecturer makes Helen jump. She has just been wondering about him, feeling a bit guilty: was he upset? Perhaps she should have gone with him. Yes, the quick, light, earnest footsteps might easily be his.

'So, he has been hovering behind me at a distance and now he's hastening in for the kill, scoring his beak through the inner skin of the egg, towards the point of my cigarette . . . No, he wouldn't follow me, it's not his way to confront his prey openly, and it would be a bit difficult for him to make a second meeting seem accidental.'

The flat shadows of the two women run towards each other along the muddy path.

. . .

When Elsie distinguishes the bright point of a lighted cigarette under the trees, her first thought is that it must belong to a man.

'One of the male students,' she concludes, as she hurries on towards the river, deciding not to look at its owner. However, when she is close, she sees that the figure with the cigarette is that of a young woman, a young woman with long hair, wearing the duffle coat and flat shoes that so many students wear, and she becomes curious. Her curiosity is aroused because, during the day, as she vacuums around the beds in the single rooms of the women's residences, Elsie creates for herself a picture of what each occupant might be like. Sometimes, the owner of the room comes in when she is in there, and then she can compare her picture of that woman with the real woman, often her imaginary picture is almost right . . . but you could never count on it. Anyway, there are still a large number of imaginary inhabitants waiting to meet the real ones and so, often, when she encounters a female student in the supermarket or at the bus-stop, she wonders to herself whether this student is one of her students, one of Elsie's students.

Elsie slackens her pace. The two shadows overlap on the path.

'Good evening,' says Elsie.

'Good evening,' replies Helen.

'Much warmer now.'

'Yes.'

That is all. Elsie walks on and her shadow disengages itself from the other shadow behind her. The two women have recognised each other.

'I thought so! That is the girl from the end room in corridor 5, B Block . . . the one with flowers in her room.'

'That is the cleaning woman who made my bed the other morning.'

. . .

The path meets the river, flowing full but clear through the evening. It's a tiny bit lighter, just a touch softer, by the river, almost as if the river were reflecting light.

'But from where? The sun disappeared over half an hour ago; and if it's not reflecting . . .' thinks Elsie, 'it must be giving off some light of its own.' She looks up and then around her to check whether the moon has risen; it might be responsible for the pale glow on the water. Above, only a few birds and one star. Behind her she sees the muffled shape of a woman, Helen sitting with her back against a tree.

'Stop dithering about, Elsie,' she says to herself, as she digs into her bag for her scarf. She bends her head, about to put it on; then, deciding against it, she hastens on her way, holding the corner of the scarf in her hand, so that it floats out beside her.

. . .

Helen gets up and stands for a moment, listening to the sound of birdsong, the evening chorus filtering through the trees. She picks up her bag and slowly walks to the river and, meeting it, turns with the path along the bank. Ahead, she sees her cleaning lady stumbling on towards the gate which opens out on to the road beside the bridge. A cleaning lady, trailing a transparent chiffon scarf like smoke.

. . .

In the second before sleep, Rebecca and Jane watch the shadowy figures of two women walking at a distance from one another, up and down on an uneven path, on the other side of the crack.

'Just one star,' Elsie checks again, reaching the gate. She steps on to the pavement.

The shadows disappear, one after the other. There is a single star shining above the crack.

SECTION 8
Flooded Yard

Dear Helen,

I did enjoy writing that section about you and Elsie. Now, it seems you are far away . . . but I'd like to tell you a bit about what has been happening on the boat.

It's been raining for several days; fine, steady rain. The river has swollen and the volume of water underneath me has greatly increased. Each morning I discover the night tide has deposited its arrangement of debris a little closer to my front door. The river is getting bold; the objects presented are larger, and this morning an enormous metal drum like a bomb stood there, confronting me from amongst the bottles, cans and assortment of old shoes, but there is plenty of driftwood for the stove. I started to make a list of the things washed in by the river; yesterday, I caught sight of a baby's bath bobbing past with the ducks. But I have given up the list: things without reason or connection, their history lost, floating downstream, and away under the stone bridge.

High tide also occurs in the late afternoon. I stare out through the rain at the water rising higher and higher into the yard. Then I notice the faces of my neighbours on the other boats at their windows and portholes, also watching. We share the same fear: that our homes will be lifted partway on to the concrete bank, so that when the river subsides, we will be left perching precariously on the edge above. Sometimes I put on my boots and paddle about in the flooded yard, vaguely testing the ropes which attach the boat to the land and checking the rusty patches in her side. At high tide the depth of the river must be more than twice the height of the boat . . . last year she sank. But that was before I came; I try not to think about it. I see that the water is full of tiny fish, little streaks like the rain.

Today it is still raining, but also windy; the wind is pushing one end of the boat out towards the middle of the river, and, when the ropes are stretched taut, the boat slams back to the wall the way a mouth snaps shut after a slow, involuntary yawn. I am sitting beside the iron cylinder of the stove, listening to the sound of the wood burning inside it; the supple sizzle and the hiss; it seems content. I feel empty. Deep inside me there is a rabbiting, itchy craving like a sexual urge. The substance of this story doesn't seem to satisfy; I can't make it storm and crackle . . . and if I don't, it will become merely a part of the drifting, will be lost in the yawn.

The stove is my life line, without it I would freeze; all the same, it's odd – this connection I have with the stove. Just now, when I stooped down to raise the little flap at the bottom, I stopped to watch the effect of the increased flow of air feeding the embers. I stayed there, bent over like a child who suddenly discovers that by hanging her head between her legs, not only can she turn the world upside down, but she can also look up, not quite but almost, inside herself; and I remembered a dream. It was a dream I had a long time ago, before I came to live on the boat or encountered the stove, in the dream I crawled up through the opening between my legs and the inside was like a dried-up old drain littered with empty tampax cartons and cigarette packets.

. . .

The letter is finished and sits on the sideboard waiting to be sent or thrown away. It is now approaching the middle of March, and, as I worry and fumble with words inside the boat, the river heaves and flows and carries my days away with it, through the rain.

. . .

'Oh days! Days, you are like clouds,' exclaims Helen, hurrying through the park, late for a lecture on Shakespeare, one bright morning.
'And we are truly mocked by
thou, "the fleeting passage of time".
But, being as 'twere
a mere puff which trills along beneath the sun,

for my lateness, I care not!
I also care not for
narrative and dramatic themes,
for sources or for structure or for
any inconsistencies of plot!
This bright morning.'

. . .

'In the sea,' says Jane, 'I had no feeling about days at all.
Just two movements: the ebb and the flow,
in which objects were rocked and nudged towards each other.
Sometimes, in the shadows, or in the moments of sunlight,
the nudged objects would touch,
sometimes not.
Whether they touched or not
did not matter.
But there were also the tiny spurts of life,
the quick darts of small fish, close to the surface.
The dash for life from A to B.
It's different now. . .'

. . .

'I don't remember the days,' says Rebecca, 'except I tried to work
and did the shopping. Then, at night, I couldn't sleep. Just lay there
awake, electric with insight, shovelling my ideas into the void.'

. . .

'Clock-strike . . . wake up, Elsie,
Clock-strike, time for work,
Clock-strike, coming for tea-break?
In between, there are little spaces,
I stop and think . . . but I let them go.
Bloody plug!' she says, struggling with the wire on the vacuum
cleaner.

. . .

A cry from Ruby:
'It's all right, I'm still moving.
Round and round on my water lily leaf
and on through the flicker of
dark tunnels and
bright stations, I orbit the world alone,
waltzing with shreds of my reflection,
chopped up
by light and now dark,
light and dark.'

. . .

Mr Smith-god is on holiday, breezing along a country lane without a care in the world.

'Aha,' he says, coming to a halt. He surveys me as if I were an insect, having landed on my back by mistake in the middle of the road, flipping my feelers in the air. 'Aha, lost again? Having to resort to poetry now?'

My poetry resort is not your holiday resort . . . I mutter something feebly; it's no use, so I continue to squirm in silence, under the shadow of a fat finger and thumb descending from the sky.

'Just a little tweak,' says Mr Smith-god with delight. (For Mr Smith-god was once very much like his apprentice, Mr Jones. In the practice of the engrossing task of killing very small things, slowly he learnt his trade, and this is still, perhaps, his greatest love.) But, when the finger touches my body, I will grab it in my tiny teeth and . . . 'Oooh, you nasty thing!' He jumps back . . . and then, luckily, he remembers that he reached a decision, only the other day, to refrain from indulging himself in this obsession of torturing small creatures . . . because, you never know, someone might be watching and label such behaviour unbecoming for one in his position.

With great relief, I watch him wander off down the road, whistling a hymn. I right myself, turn the page and continue on my way.

SECTION 9
Treading into Amazing Curving

Dusk, through which the shining liquid in the crack winds its way to the sea; its light ebbs lower and is gone. Dark. In the dark, a faint breeze steals across miles of distance, barely brushing the surface of the invisible land.

I hear the voice of a woman leap out of the night, calling, 'Rebecca, Rebecca' . . . Rebecca has gone, the old woman has disappeared . . . and so has the cat. The cry is followed from the same source, by the sound of sobbing: 'Something is lost, is lost in the dark.'

As her sobbing subsides, Jane lays herself down on the earth and attempts to wrap the darkness around her. But the darkness is still and will not be wrapped. It is distance as well as darkness, and, even if she could move beyond it, she wouldn't be nearer anyone or the nameless part of herself which is lost. When she has thrown all power of hope of finding the part that is lost into the darkness and found no response, when the acquisitive spirit in the darkness has run away with all that is precious and turned its back on her, refusing to muffle her pain with sleep, Jane lies wide awake staring up at black space, on the battleground of the lonely. Her eyes are blankly fixed on the dim gleam of a solitary star; she is waiting.

The dark intelligence in the dark applies the familiar instruments of torture to her body with care. In a series of precise movements her body is being eased apart, limb from limb, gently, as if the flux of pain spreading into the gaps between the joints were to be weighed and measured. Her body does not break.

She screws up her eyes in a desperate effort to squeeze a route out through the dark and, in a flash, burning red pressure is being applied to her temples; two flat, red-hot irons placed either side of her head are searing through her hair and her skin. She wrenches

73

her body away, raises herself on her knees and screams and screams into the dark: 'Rebecca! Rebecca!' The screams for help are in vain; as useless as the cries of a seal barking beneath the blows of a hunter's club in the land of perpetual night. And Jane takes up the hunter's weapon and turns it against her herself, hitting her own head with her own clenched fists, hard, to deaden the pressure from the irons. The pressure is increased.

As she sinks down, the old pain, the oldest pain of all, which she has been sheltering inside her, is slowly exposed; as if a ribbon of bandage were being unwound and pulled out from between her legs, leaving a fine piece of metal, sharp as the thin lid of a tin can, cutting, cutting, lacerating her womb from inside. The creeping sickness begins to uncoil itself in the pit of her stomach . . . and Mr Smith-god, if you dare, if you dare butt in here now, I will smash you in the face with my fists . . . but, I remember, I have tried that once and it does not work.

. . .

The full moon rises quickly from the sea, shedding pale light on to her daughter Jane; she sways her light into the darkness with the rhythm of one carrying a lantern across the dunes of a desert in the night. Jane feels a smooth sadness ripple over her; the pain in her womb shifts a little, and slowly from the crack between her legs, blood begins to drip.

The wavering light of the moon washes the tree into view and limply, bravely, Jane crawls towards it. Lying before the tree, with her face to the ground, she reaches out her aching arms; her hands feel for one another behind the trunk, touch and hold in a definite clasp. For a long time, she remains motionless, like a star talisman hanging on to a string around the neck of the world. The earth about her is textured with moonlight and spotted with blood. Then she pulls herself up, wraps her dressing-gown around her knees and sits with her back against the tree, beside the crack, looking out over the plain.

The force of the darkness has been heaved up and forged by the glow from the moon into a dome, secured by the bright points of many stars. She sees that the flat surface of the land is alive with

74

moving shadows. Certain sea creatures, such as herring, migrate with the full moon; this is a migration across the earth. The silent beings flowing in waves across the plain are women. Souls from another place moving across this place, their heads bent low. Women burnt, stoned, tortured for witchcraft. Mutilated women with bleeding wombs, 'mad' women suffocated in mental hospitals, sacrificed slave women, footbound women hobbling on rotting feet. Wives who have said nothing and have not lived, wives who have spoken and had their tongues torn out. Women in pictures hung on walls around the world: the starlets, the cuties, the pin-up girls. Women dragging chains and chastity belts. The raped girl children, the raped young women, the raped middle-aged women, the raped old women . . . the whores, the bitches, the broads, the hags, the cunts, the spinsters, the sissies. . . In their midst, a slight figure, faceless, hardly discernible; the shadow of Ruby glides across the plain. They pass, with sorrow and with dignity, on their way to the sea under the bleeding moon.

The full moon spreads up on silver wings into the night, up and over the tree, on a spinning journey of many years, many lives, sinks and then drops out of sight through an invisible door in the sky. She leaves behind her a profound stillness like a blessing, left in a place by one who departs for those who will follow on.

. . .

The moon, the stars, the shadows of the women, have gone. Jane is sitting in silence under the tree. As the first rays from the sun clamber out of the sea, the bright sound of a bird singing begins to chip into the silence above her: 'Yes, there are, yes, there are,' it chips. She looks up: yes, there are . . . there are leaves on the branches. She has been feeling so much a part of the still morning haze . . . but now all around her the stillness is cracking and, peering through its chinks, she sees the quickening of the day. At first she does not understand.

For the sun this day is dawning over a landscape no longer flat. The expanse ahead of her, to her left and to her right, has been etched into curving shape by the paths of the women, trodden like contours into the earth during the night. The bands of colour in the fabric of the surface are now all wrinkled and swirly. She continues to look, in half-belief . . . her vision tiptoeing over the grassy mounds of hills, through dark clumps of trees, pausing and peeping until it is thrown back, by virtue of bumping into the rocky feet belonging to an extremely tall range of mountains, standing at the western edge.

'The air is perfectly clear,' she whispers to herself, sitting, watching; and the stillness erupts into a fanfare of birdsong. This is followed by a terrific rumble. Jane hangs on to the roots of the tree, transfixed, as the pink mountains in the west bow and kneel together in a line. Now, driving their strong knees forward into the earth, they lean back on their haunches and fling up their proud heads to the sun. And the sunlight anoints them and runs off their shoulders, down crimson creases into the lap of their skirts, highlighting the patterning of streams, the threads of blue lakes woven into their hems, with a dazzling extravagance. The light is then caught in the soft bowl of the plain and flows easily amongst the hills, trees, the caves and the fields, spilling at length into the crack. When all is calm, Jane suddenly wonders if the change has been carried over to the other side. She turns sharply and is disappointed.

On the other side of the crack a change has taken place, but it is very slight – pathetic in comparison with what she has just been looking at. The curtain of mist has retreated a little, so that she can see a sallow shore and a few straggles of vegetation, but apart from this the grey mist curtain remains closed as blankly and as sternly as before. However, it seems that the gulf created by the crack has widened considerably, and looking across the shining liquid now is more like looking out to the shore of another country, rather than merely over to the farther bank of a river. The liquid in the crack is flowing more strongly, with greater confidence, but the effect of the breach is strangely disquietening. And when she turns again to face the plain, for a second she has the eerie feeling that she is clinging, clinging to the rim of a huge green bowl which is wheeling, detached and lonely, through the air. Then her hand touches something moist in the grass; her fingers are red at the tips, tinged with her own menstrual blood.

'I wonder where Mr Smith-god is today!' says Rebecca, walking up the slope towards her.

'I don't know, I haven't seen him,' Jane replies.

. . .

In fact, Mr Smith-god has been there for quite a while. During all the activity of sunlight on the plain, he has been attempting to send up flares of his own sombre light. It is, however, even for the most discerning eye, difficult to distinguish him . . . the forlorn shape of a bedraggled camper, crouching somewhere in the mountains, trying to light a flare in the drizzle with a box of damp matches. It is true that several of the matches do flicker for a moment, but only to illuminate his own furious face as if in spite. At length, he is forced to give up the attempt and stomps off in a rage, leaving behind him a little trail of burnt-out matches, little lines which don't connect, down the far side of the mountains.

. . .

Rebecca throws herself down beside Jane at the foot of the tree. 'Isn't it amazing!' she says.

'Yes.'

'Jane. . .' She looks at her; it is obvious that Jane isn't listening, just sitting in silence with her legs straight in front of her, palms flat on the grass. Her hair is hanging down her back, her face seems so young, her expression is receptive, open, alert.

'You're right,' thinks Rebecca, 'any comment on the "view" would be ridiculous.' Rebecca relaxes and allows herself, too, to become totally absorbed into the movement of the liquid flowing down the crack and into the stillness in that movement which reaches deeper than still water as it merges with the distance, creating the space for silence; melting, infusing, distilling, until even the sun becomes a golden bubble being borne lightly across the blue.

'There are so many lies,' says Jane, abruptly.

'What do you mean?'

'I can't say exactly. You weren't here last night. Where were you? Rebecca, I saw many, many women, thousands of women, walking

77

here, across the plain and everything changed. And they left behind this silence. This silence isn't empty, it's full. It's real, Rebecca, it's real.' She stands up, frustrated and excited, feeling that she is holding a glowing truth in her hands, that no one else will ever be able to see, and that she might as well simply dash it to the floor.

'Hang on,' says Rebecca, 'I'm not disagreeing with you!'

'That's not the point . . . whether you agree or disagree. Do you understand?'

'I think so. When I was painting, sometimes it seemed a bit like that,' says Rebecca, earnestly fidgeting strands of her hair back behind her ears, as if the hair in her face were somehow impeding her attempt to articulate a complicated, intangible feeling. Jane sits down.

'It seemed to go in several stages. For the first few years everything was fine, I was completely bound up in the business of being a painter, which meant . . . you know, hours and hours spent drinking beer in smoke-filled pubs, trying to talk louder than anyone else. It all seemed very important, we were discussing "art"! But, whenever I felt I was really getting anywhere, saying something that I actually meant, I would always be pulled back by cries of "Come on, you don't really mean that," and it would be turned into a joke, and we would all have another drink. Do you know what it was like? It was like there were a lot of people at the bottom of a hole with slippery sides, and we were pulling each other down all the time in separate attempts to get out to the sky; to something. Then one day I walked in, and there they are all were in the corner, debating as loudly as usual, and it looked really cosy. Suddenly, I realised that that was all they wanted really; they wanted the sky out of reach, and all the scrabbling was enjoyable to them. They didn't *want* to get anywhere! It made me really angry. I walked out. I stopped going to pubs.'

'Didn't they wonder about you?'

'Well, I suppose so; they used to phone up and stuff like that, but they soon stopped . . . Anyway, then I became a sort of "anti-artist". It was really exciting at first, as if I was running off down a solitary tunnel, tearing into the notion of "art" all on my own. I bought lots of really outrageous clothes and redecorated my

78

studio all in white . . . but then it was like I lost sight of the sky altogether, and gradually everything became painful and lonely and dark.'

Jane screws her eyes together in an effort to understand what the other woman is saying. 'What do you mean, dark?'

'Well, I was so furious and everything I was doing seemed totally meaningless, so everything I painted, I would look at, then immediatley I tore it up, until I had nothing left. In the end it occurred to me that it was all the questions which were wrong. So every time "why?" cropped up, I pushed it down with my foot, like a ledge to help me up. Things started getting a bit clearer.'

'But "why?" is important.'

'Of course, it was down there it was wrong, it was just pretending; false . . .'

'And then?'

'Well, I felt I was getting closer to something, but the trouble was it seemed to have nothing to do with anyone else in the world! . . . whether I was a painter for "art" or "anti-art" didn't really matter. It was like the world was completely blank, looking at me blankly . . . no wonder my friends spent so much time clinging to each other in the pub! Anyway, I gave up and went and got a job in an office, might as well become part of the blankness, I thought . . . at least it's being part of something.'

Jane laughs. 'I'm sorry,' she says, 'it's just the idea of you in an office, lurking behind a typewriter, disguised as "part of the blankness"!'

'It didn't last long. One night I was biking home, and it dawned on me how stupid that was . . . that, of course, there must be something behind all these questions, beyond the blankness, you know . . . some kind of truth.' She glances at Jane. Jane isn't laughing.

'Which came from where?'

'Well, it is strange, it came from colour, initially. I realised that there is no such thing really. No, what I mean is that there are two sorts of colour: dead colour and living colour. All this time I had been using dead colour to create . . . no wonder everything I made was artificial! That's why I hated what I was doing and what I saw

79

everyone else doing around me, and all those conversations in the pub; it was the tone, the tone which was false. I began to see living colour as always changing . . . that's what I mean by there being no such thing as colour; it's not static. I saw that light and shape could lend to yellow its own yellowness, and that yellow could speak, no, not speak . . . sing.'

She pauses, looking out in front of her. Jane waits.

'And that is similar to what you were saying, Jane, about silence not being empty, isn't it? The truth is right there in the yellowness . . . it's not in the idea or the activity of painting something yellow . . . that's just covering up, the opposite . . . Do you follow me?'

'I think so. What does the yellow sing?'

'Oh, it depends . . . different things, millions of things . . . yellow glory, yellow joy, yellow pain . . . it doesn't just sing; it rings, it burns.

'Anyway, that was the first time I really felt committed . . . to something that was outside and inside myself at the same time, and I really wanted to fight for it, to open it out this . . . this truth. But you're right, it's then you see all the lies. Suddenly I saw everything as being covered up, everywhere there were lies closing in and distorting. So it was like I could see, but I couldn't bear to look and it seemed as if the lies were going to win, and I would be labelled "lunatic" and locked away. . .'

'And now?'

On the branches of the tree there are leaves. Quietly, the cat stalks up the grass slope and takes her place beside the two women. They sit in silence, looking out across the curving plain, and the silence is colourful.

SECTION 10

Helen, Elsie and the Vacuum

Something bright; the sun, pressing through the thin mud green curtains, wakes her up. Through the focus of its rays, Helens discerns a naked male form by the window, pulling at a heap of clothes on the floor. Aware of her gaze, the naked man becomes uneasy and turns away. He dresses himself hurriedly. Once dressed, he walks towards her in the bed, dispersing the specks of dust trapped in the sunlight.

His head bows over her. She feels that the room is revolving curiously, round and round, as if they are sinking under water.

'Are you very late?' she says.

'No, it's OK . . . the seminar never starts on time. See you for lunch . . . I'll think about you.' The form retreats, shutting the door carefully.

The room re-establishes itself into an upright position by way of a long, sidling somersault and balances slowly. Helen sits up and reaches out to the bedside table for a cigarette. Smoking the cigarette somehow seems to complete the experience of the night before – dissolving its mystery, releasing it into the air. After a while, she picks up this book and reads . . . 'Out on the plain . . .' She stops.

'I'm not going to read anymore of this!' she says. 'And if I were you, I wouldn't bother to write anymore, either! It's so incredibly precious and one-sided. All the faults you ascribe to Mr Smith-god and Mr Jones you commit yourself. I don't feel as if I'm "out on the plain" with you. I don't want to be there, being dragged around by your inflated words and clung on to, pulled back and forth at your convenience and denied my own existence! I don't believe in it in the slightest and, what's more, I don't think you do either . . . It's a game, a pretence and it's just as selfish and devouring as, as . . .

D. H. Lawrence!'

Her face is white in the yellow light.

' "Her" face happens to be my face, and I don't want it described in your book!' she screams.

'It's not "she screams"; it's "I scream" . . . Helen, me!'

OK. "I scream." My pen scrawls the words into the page . . . now it isn't clear who is screaming . . .

'So what? Anyway, we are both screaming . . . two screaming women in a room in a university residence, in the morning . . . who cares?'

Helen, what is it?

'Don't be stupid . . . you know quite well what took place here last night; that I slept here with a *man*. Well, I wanted to, I needed to, I enjoyed it. And I felt so safe with him; it was such a relief from all this intensity, this bond between women, this hysterical swooping amongst the stars! All that is so blinding and fierce . . . and I don't want it! This man is important to me, and now, if you don't mind, I want to think about lunchtime and seeing him again . . . but, oh no, you do mind and so here you are, creeping about like a relentless, spying parasite, to call me a traitor. And for all your talk about freedom and truth, it's not really anything open or free you want at all; that's just a cover up, an attempt to compensate for your own failure to have any worthwhile relationships . . . all the time, from behind your banner of openness, you are screaming attack . . . attack, attack all men!'

But, Helen, I'm trying to write about women's consciousness; of course, my own experience comes into that, but the discovery that I don't feel a failure without a man, that in fact I enjoy my own company, is a discovery which I think I share with many women. Although it's something comparatively new for me, I don't assume that I am special . . . I think this is a knowledge which women have always had deep down, something which has been hidden from us by men.

'Bloody hell . . . do you know what you sound like? Can you hear the tone in that? It's so condescending! I can hardly believe you dare write it! You commit the crime in precisely the same way that Lawrence does . . . first you deny any independent striving to the opposite sex, being totally obsessed by the way they have affected your own precious self; then you try to herd the whole of your own sex together under your skirts, so that we all have to think the same as you. Oh yes, I can just see it; Lawrence and you; children sitting in the playroom opposite each other; he is stuffing his toy soldiers into a red phallic shaped cushion and you are stuffing your dolls into another cushion . . . you don't even know what shape yours is, except that it's got a crack in it! Every now and again you hold a little boxing bout in which you biff each other with your stuffed pillows, but not to hurt, because you need each other intact, so that you can repeat the performance over and over again. If you ask me, it's all totally pathetic and contrived.'

. . .

So, I put down my pen and run away from the page to my appointment at the hairdresser's. The young woman at the hairdresser's informs me that my hair is already too short, but she will do her best to make it look feminine. I stare abuse at myself in the mirror whilst she clips away at my hair. I answer her matter-of-fact questions about my life in monosyllables.

. . .

Helen turns over in bed, sobbing, her need for him rising like a thin cry through her blank heavy tears. This need for him is so sharp that she feels it must be capable of cutting through the distance between them to the sunless cell at the bottom of the arts block, where she pictures him, one in a circle of bored students, his head bent over a book. Then she imagines that, suddenly, he becomes aware of her cry, peers out of the window and sees her perching like a lonely bird on a tree outside; and so he gets up, excuses himself, nods his way out of the circle to the door and flies quickly to her side. And she, the lonely bird, nestles up close to him, warm brother bird, on the branch, and they face the day together. But when, in her imagination, he inclines his gentle head with its bright eye towards her to ask her what is wrong, and she starts to tell him about how she has been chased by feminists, feminists like cats, way out into a strange, unknown country and been torn at and snatched at . . . she sees his bright eye slowly become dim. It is as if that eye were shielded by an inner lid which finally shuts off what it does not want to see. Then, not unkindly, he pulls her towards him, eagerly ruffling up her feathers with his beak . . . and she feels annoyed and distant and so alone again inside . . .

She has stopped crying, distracted like a child by her own story, but when her story stops, she pulls the sheet over her head and starts to cry again. Even the sun is hateful: intense and gobbling.

The door opens, a hand thrusts a vacuum cleaner into the room and withdraws. The abandoned machine stands forlornly in the sunlight. Helen takes no notice. There is the sound of footsteps scuttling away along the hard corridor . . . and back.

'Oh, I'm sorry.'

Helen peels back the sheet and peeps over its edge at Elsie in her brown overall, standing in the doorway.

'It doesn't matter, come in,' says Helen. Then she ducks back under the sheet and resumes her conversation with herself in silence: 'Nothing matters, let her come in and push her sucking vacuum cleaner around. What does it matter that the room is perfectly clean already? Just a stupid cleaning woman playing her part; clearing the way for the inevitable dance of the day. No, not the dance; procession . . . our daily procession in and out of little cells, along concrete paths and back again . . . tramping and plodding in the vacuum.'

She grips the sheet down tighter over her head and listens to the vacuum cleaner purring with gratification as it is pushed around the room by Elsie's hand, sucking nothing contentedly into nothing. Then she becomes impatient with the noise and waits angrily for it to stop and shrink away. But it continues, sucking, sucking like the sun through the window. She is conscious that the bedspread has fallen off the bed, that her body is lying naked beneath the meagre protection of the sheet, and the sunlight is penetrating through the sheet . . . the buzzing and the sucking and the bumping of the vacuum cleaner across the floor become louder. A chair is scraped out from under the desk, banging against a leg. 'Whoops!' a tiny sound escapes from the lips of the cleaning woman, like a bird across the sky.

'All I want is nothing, but not your nothing,' whispers Helen to herself, as softly the tears begin to flow again. Another bump, this time against the side of the bed . . . then quiet. In the silence Helen offers up her spirit to the sun: 'Take this frail shape, I give up . . .'

Nothing happens, she is still a frail shape trembling under a sheet, like an animal on the point of being discovered under a dock leaf, waiting for the end. If she had been an animal discovered by Mr Smith-god like this, frail and shivering in the undergrowth, and he happened to be in a hurry, he would have shot her dead in an instant and thought nothing of it. And, in this instance, Mr Smith-god would have been unknowingly perpetrating an act of kindness . . . well, one could almost say that for this particular short-sighted moment. However, the hand which now taps gingerly on the thin dock leaf-sheet roof does not belong to Mr Smith-god.

Helen is reluctant to uncurl herself from under the sheet.

'What's the matter, love?' says Elsie. She had been unable to avoid noticing that Helen's face was red, streaked with tears, when she first came in. It was worrying about this that had made her so clumsy with the vacuum cleaner.

'It's nothing,' mumbles Helen. Then she grins at the irony of its all being nothing.

'Sorry, I didn't mean to be so noisy, love.' Elsie takes a few steps towards the door, wishing she had not said anything. It is probably best to go; perhaps the student thinks she is being nosy. Part of her wants to stay and give comfort: to mother, to cover the pain, to wipe it all away . . . but that doesn't seem quite right here.

Helen sits up in bed. 'I don't know,' she says, shrugging her shoulders. With relief she feels the pain slither obediently down inside her; she is being 'grown up' about it. 'I think I want to go home,' she says.

'Is it boyfriend trouble?'

'No, well yes . . . not really. It's just me and this place.'

'Don't you like it?'

'No, I hate it.'

'Oh.' The emphasis on the word 'hate' strikes Elsie forcibly. She had known students, of course, to be unhappy before and had always tried to imagine reasons for this . . . perhaps they had fallen out with somebody or were not getting on too well with their work. When she saw them again, the next day or maybe a few days later, they seemed happy enough. It was true that one or two had left, but this was unusual. In the blunt statement, 'I hate it,' there is a sort of lump which she can't quite smooth away. 'Yes, so do I,' she says with equal bluntness.

'It must be worse for you.'

'Oh, I don't think about it much; it's just a way of earning my bread and butter.'

'Would you like a cigarette?' says Helen.

They both light cigarettes. Elsie gathers up the bedspread from the floor and drapes it back over the sheet, before sitting down on the edge of the bed.

'How long have you been working here?' asks Helen.

'Ten years . . . I came when it first opened.'

'Are you going to stay?'

'I haven't got much choice. Anyway, it's not bad, but I don't know . . . sometimes I think I would like to move away; to Spain or somewhere like that. But John would never leave his job, and there's Diane and Peter. I never mention it.'

'Who are they?'

'John is my husband, and Diane and Peter are my children; well, they are in their teens now. John works in the plastics factory.'

'Elsie . . . Elsie . . .' A high-pitched voice calls along the corridor outside. Elsie looks at her watch.

'Better go, it's teabreak. Don't worry love . . . you won't be here forever.' She stubs out her cigarette, stands up and straightens the creases in the nylon skin of her brown overall.

'Bye . . . thanks,' says Helen.

Then Elsie pushes the flabby vacuum cleaner out of the room and closes the door. 'Coming,' she shouts, and Helen listens to her footsteps receding chink, chink, over the hard floor and the faint wisp, wisp, of the nylon overall rubbing against itself. These small sounds are soon absorbed into the chorus of laughter which is issuing forth from the changing rooms at the end of the corridor, where the cleaning women assemble to drink their morning tea out of thermos flasks.

'No time to think now.' Helen draws her knees up under her chin and gives herself a little hug. Then, she gets out of bed, dresses, stuffs some books from her desk into her bag, opens the curtains and finally launches herself out of the room, off into the vacuum; bravely, in response to the spinning sun, which has now withdrawn to a respectable distance.

SECTION 11
Air

One morning towards the end of March, I get up, select a skirt and a jumper from the heap of clothes at the end of the bed and put them on. My cat races past me along the little corridor to the kitchen, where we were greeted by a pile of dirty dishes stacked in the sink. I rummage around amongst them for the bent fork which I use for the cat's food and dollop some meaty jelly out of a can on to her plate. She doesn't eat her food, but sits by the front door, as usual, waiting for me. I deposit the fork back in the sink.

I open the door and as I step out on to the land I am hit full in the face by a blast of warmth. We stand beside one another, the cat and I, stunned and still sleepy, blinking and puzzled; it is as if the boat had borne us away from England during the night and we had just stepped out into a harbour in the tropics. But, of course, we are in the same old boatyard; the transformation which occurred during the night is due to the entire displacement of chilled air. We accept this as a fact, and trot off over the gangplanks, the cat sniffing, leading the way across the shining water to the wooden hut, where the letters are delivered into a communal letterbox.

I collect my letters and the cat escorts me back. As I bend down to jump on board again, I glance across the river to the trees on the other side; at the tips of their branches I see a splattering of fresh green.

. . .

There is a tray on the table beside me. On the tray are my two letters propped against the full teapot, a cup, and toast on a plate. Sunlight is falling diagonally across the room from the window in the corner. The cat is in the kitchen eating her breakfast.

As I drink my tea, I contemplate the change in the weather. For such a long time I have been aware of the growing pressure, as I have sat here forcing words up through the grey, dark days and the cold, and suddenly, the pressure has burst; it's warm outside. The longed for change, now that it is here, is almost frightening. The secret, underground growth is exposed, and I'm afraid that my words might float up and disappear in the new, clear air. But there are green leaves attached securely to the trees . . . and I suppose I will have to carry my words around with me like that, like leaves balanced on the top of my head, now that the pressure inside has been released . . .

The change inside has been accompanied by the change outside or, rather, it is the other way round . . . but whichever way round it is, one doesn't notice it happen. It's annoying how most important changes occur out of sight, during the night or behind our backs, without our being able to see the complete pattern, the combining and mingling of forces which create a change . . . and the change itself, the exact moment of transition, evades us. Even when I have stayed up all night to watch the dawn, somehow I have missed it. I always happen to be looking at the ground or become distracted by the rustle of a bird in the undergrowth or be lighting a cigarette and I miss the precise point when the first beat from the sun rushes into the irresolute lull before dawn . . . I only witness the second beat. During the months of sadness in my life, however carefully I have plotted my journey across that sadness, thinking: today I am happier, today I am more confident, tomorrow I will be . . . I can never say; it is happening now, it is now that my left foot is lifting off the last sad stepping stone and my right foot is touching the land. It's only when I have been on the land for quite a while that I realise that I am no longer sad and then, looking back, I feel strangely detached from the little string of stepping stones left in the water behind me.

Yesterday the air was white and thick . . . today it is clear and bright. I pour my tea . . . it's as if the young dawn, tiptoeing towards this particular day, discovered a torn seam in the cold cloth which wraps itself securely around the northen hemisphere in winter; stealthily, she parted the seam and squeezed through, spreading herself out joyfully over the world in the space underneath.

I crunch into my toast, sip my tea and read my letters in the sun-filled boat. Helen is waiting in a room at the top of the arts block for a lecture on Thomas Hardy to begin; this book is open on her knees. Somewhere my friends, who have written the letters, who will someday, perhaps, read these words, are moving about amongst people in rooms, at work; and, suddenly, I realise that somewhere, somewhere there is a silent, unknown woman, sitting reading, who looks up from the page and gives me no indication of what she is thinking. 'Out on the plain' . . . I'm never sure what is happening there during the time I am away.

. . .

At the mention of the word 'time' Mr Smith-god's face brightens, then he assumes a severe expression. 'Time, gentlemen, please.' He pounds his fist down on to a beer-smeared counter; Mr Jones anxiously taps his watch.

'Doing your time!' Mr Smith-god slams the prison gates shut.

'Time will run out! Ha, ha,' he cries . . . But he is struggling with a most 'untimely' crisis of identity: not quite knowing whether he is the landlord of a pub, the policeman in the street, the warden at a prison, the adjudicator presiding over an examination . . . or the husband in charge of watching sand drizzle through a little glass instrument whilst his wife boils an egg. I turn and address him with stern formality: Mr Smith-god, you are dismissed. He is so confused that he gratefully accepts an order from me and wanders off stupidly, like one having received a medal, out of a crowded hall.

. . .

Today is an air day, and we can use the air to get to the plain. Shut your eyes.

'That's a bit difficult to do,' says Helen, 'seeing as I am supposed to be reading the words!'

I can hear my friends cackling, lifting my cap of earnest intensity for a moment . . . Come on, I say, clasping the cap firmly back down on to my head.

'Squashing the elaborately burgeoning display of words like leaves!'

What?

'Words like leaves,' says Helen. 'A few paragraphs back you informed us that you have a crop of words like leaves balanced on top of your head. I'm surprised you have a cap which fits on top of all that lot! . . . Sorry.'

Oh, come on, at least you can try, just for the spirit of spring! I shut my eyes, still writing, and I can feel the words running out of my pen, sprouting in all directions across the page. I am writing an air poem which is to be read upwards, starting from the bottom of the next page . . .

Open eyes.
a song
are inside
as if you
You rise,
airstack.
up, up the
noses you
as the rhythm
higher, you float
stretching out,
You relax,
flowers and balances on top of breath.
Controlled breath
up from underneath it.
Forcing another out and
to rest.
circles and comes
blossoms up, squeezed out from the one already there,
Each breath an impulse
you up.
Clear breaths swinging
you touch nothing.
As you spread out your arms and legs,
into the airstack of breaths.
float up now on the first layer of air
Get ready,
Close your eyes.
. . . *Here*.

. . . Open your eyes, and read your way down, tumbling back to the bottom of the page. Try again, up . . . spreading out flat, balanced on wafting layers of air which support your weight, you rest and look down.

'Come down, come down at once!' shouts Mr Smith-god from below, shaking his fist at the sky. 'You are mad.' He is an indignant grey dot which quivers and stamps a tiny black foot on the ground.

. . .

Helen gazes around the room at the top of the arts block, at her fellow students and the lecturer now assembled. The lecturer is mouthing words to which no one is listening; the students are occupied in drawing doodles on their foolscap writing pads. She returns to this book, lying open on her knees under the desk, and climbs to the top of the poem once more. It is quite easy for her to slip out of the window unnoticed. She spreads out her arms and her legs, lifting away from the peak of the poem.

Flying. When she feels at ease, confident that the layers of air beneath her will not collapse, Helen opens her eyes. She steers on easily through clear blue sky, between slanting shafts of sunlights. At a great distance below she sees the heads of purple mountains, the glint of lakes, then hills, fields, woods. But it is the invisible power of which she is most aware, the power living underneath the landscape, pushing and stretching the fabric of the surface, creating the rises of its curves, its plunging valleys, slowly, on and on, in silence. The dashes of bright colour and the variations in texture which clothe the form seem very, very temporary, like rippling notions or echoes from an older, deeper consciousness.

Carefully, she follows the form of the land which creases into the golden crack . . . and beyond. All of a sudden she feels giddy, for beyond the crack she can see nothing but a great cloud of vacant mist which seems to want to absorb her down out of the clear air into a murky blur. She is losing her balance, about to fall . . .

Her eyes cling steadfastly to the line of the crack, and again she is gliding safely, buoyed up on the shimmering layers of air. She navigates her vision along the crack, snaking and looping through the network of colour, to the shore, where it floods gold into blue;

green sea. And there, far out over the waves, she can just make out a lonely spot, circled in silver, rotating slowly; the sunshine highlights a golden head, and the ruby tips of fingers waving . . .

. . .

'You are doing it again!' says Helen, out of the blue . . . literally!
What?
'You are speaking my lines for me.'
I can't help it sometimes.
'That's obvious!'
We are supposed to be doing this together, you know.
Instead of answering, she swoops away over the tree tops.

. . .

There is a spontaneous shuffling of papers in the room at the top of the arts block, signifying that the lecture is over. The lecturer struts out of the door, the students push down the corridor to the lift. Helen closes this book and lands with a bump on the ground.

Rebecca and Jane are suddenly aware of a female figure in blue jeans and blue jumper striding crossly towards them down a nearby hill, her hair flying out behind her.

'This is the most ridiculous part I have ever been called upon to play in my life,' mutters the figure to herself. 'I was going to the coffee bar and meet Phillip . . . and now I am dragged out here.'

It's your choice.

'Not really . . . OK, to an extent it is, but I'm only doing it for your sake, you know . . . because you wouldn't know what to write about next if I didn't.'

It's true I don't know what to write about next, but your being out on the plain doesn't make it any easier!

'Oh well,' says Helen, forgetting me, 'I suppose there always has to be someone to step out on to the moon or be the first to emerge from the primeval forest or discover the wheel!' She looks up. A woman swathed in orange and green has jumped up and is waving at her furiously from underneath a tree.

'Hello,' yells Rebecca.

There is another woman in a pale garment hanging on to the skirts of the jumping woman.

'Calm down,' says Jane. But Rebecca, who will not calm down, skids down the little slope and is now running across the grass towards Helen.

'Hello, Rebecca,' shouts Helen to the rapidly approaching figure.

'How do you know my name?' says Rebecca, reaching her.

'I . . . read about you in a book,' says Helen, uneasily.

'That's crazy! No one has ever written a book about me!'

'I know it's crazy. All the same, I'm surprised you didn't realise. I feel it all the time, this constant manipulation . . . being shoved around from one scene to another; I'm in it, too, you see.'

Rebecca laughs. 'What's your part like, then?'

'Pretty bad,' says Helen, feeling increasingly awkward. 'I sort of started off as a reader and before I knew where I was, I found myself included as a character, called upon every now and again to discuss the work in progress . . . I'm only here now because she has got lost,' she adds.

'Who is "she"?'

'Oh, just a woman in a houseboat who scribbles down words.'

Puzzled silence.

'Well, as far as I am concerned,' says Rebecca definitely, 'I got here on my own.'

As they walk back across the plain towards Jane, who is sitting under the tree stroking the cat, I can almost see clamours of disbelief from every quarter rising like flames out of the crack . . . But somewhere there is a silent reader . . . and the silent reader reads on . . . I, too, must have faith.

. . .

Jane watches the two women advance towards her. She bends over and fiddles with the buckle on her sandal. She is thinking how easy it must be to be Rebecca, who could meet anyone, it seemed, and immediately have something to say . . . whereas she always wanted to run away. Why couldn't it have been her, Jane, who had run forward to greet the stranger who had appeared over the hill, saying simply, 'Hello, I'm Jane, this is Rebecca'? Now, the order has been established; Rebecca first, and she the shadow, the indistinct woman, second. It was like being at school: whenever she had made a friend, a real friend who she could give things to, suddenly, one of the other girls in the class would quarrel with her friend and, looking around for a new companion, would seize Jane's best friend from her, leaving Jane with the other one, the other castoff. So the two rejected ones would sit together at the front of the class pretending to get on with their work, whilst the other two sat at the back and giggled. After a week or two, the girl who Jane was now sitting next to, would get fed up and make friends, quite unexpectedly, with a new girl . . . or join the other two at the back. Then followed months in which Jane was alone, waiting for a shift in the combinations of friends, until, at last, someone was left out and would be forced to approach her. In bed at night, she lay awake in the dark making lists, murmuring names to herself:

'Jackie and Gaynor,

Carol and Michelle,

Jenny and Mary . . .'

She developed the murmur into a chant, introducing her own name whenever she felt inclined . . . 'Jenny and Jane' . . . like a spell.

'This is Jane,' says Rebecca. Jane looks up into the faces of the two women standing above her.

'I'm Helen,' announces the new woman.

'Rebecca and Jane,

Jane and Rebecca,

Rebecca and Helen,

Helen and Rebecca,

Helen and Rebecca . . .'

. . . the chant unwinds inside Jane, the spell working backwards against her.

'Helen reckons we are all characters in a book!' says Rebecca, sitting down on the grass beside Jane. 'What do you think about that, then?'

Jane can't think of anything to say. She couldn't say 'that's interesting', or 'that's nice', which are the only two phrases which come to mind. Probably, this is supposed to be a joke.

'What do you mean?' she says in the end.

'I'm not quite sure,' says Helen. 'That's what I thought . . . but I don't know, I can't explain.'

There is silence.

'Anyway, it's not a bad place to find oneself in,' says Rebecca.

'No, it's really beautiful,' responds Helen eagerly, anxious to get away from the subject of their being characters in a book. 'I saw it from the air. It was lovely looking down on it, really colourful . . . but it is even better being in it.'

Rebecca jerks her head towards Helen and frowns. 'From the air?'

'Oh dear! I must seem absolutely mad,' thinks Helen, plucking at the grass. 'Well, how did you get here?' she says, at last.

'I can't remember,' says Rebecca. She is beginning to feel uneasy herself. 'I'm hungry.'

'That's something that did occur to me,' says Helen. 'It's all very well, all this dancing and prancing about out here and watching the light fall down over the hills . . . but what do you eat?'

'I don't know,' says Rebecca. She turns to Jane.

Jane shrugs her shoulders. 'Never felt hungry here before.'

'That means,' continues Helen, 'unless you don't need to eat here, you must go somewhere else to eat . . . so you are not here all the time!'

'What is happening is awfully odd,' thinks Jane. 'We arrived here, I can't remember where from . . . and yet when Rebecca was talking about her painting and her friends in the pub it all seemed perfectly natural, I knew what she was talking about, I could see it happening. And the chant, the names? I can visualise them, too, Jackie and Gaynor . . . I know what they looked like . . .'

Rebecca speaks. 'I know that, once, since I've been here, I had the feeling that I had "stepped back" or rather that I simply had not been here for a while . . . I thought that was just because I had been asleep. It was when the landscape changed shape during the night, you know, when I walked up to the tree and found you sitting and looking at it all, Jane.'

'You definitely weren't here that night,' says Jane, 'not as you,' she adds, rather surprised at her own assertion, 'but you did have a part in changing the landscape.'

'What do you mean?' says Rebecca.

The women stare at the small patch of ground between them anxiously, as if they can see the shape of the conversation there, in the grass, like the heavy head of a flower swinging up to the daylight, clinging on to a frail stalk which seems hardly able to bear its weight.

'I can't say at the moment,' says Jane.

Helen looks out across the plain. 'I don't understand, either. I have been watching everything that happens here from somewhere else . . . by reading it in a book, it was just words. Those words would be there, are still there, inside the covers of the book, whether I read them or not, but . . .'

Rebecca looks up as well: 'This place would be here, whether we came or not,' she says.

'No,' says Helen, 'I don't think it would altogether. I mean, of course, it would exist, but only as the other side of somewhere else.'

'A shadow land,' says Rebecca.

'Yes,' says Helen enthusiastically, 'you know how the moon always looks . . . sad and vague? That's because she is seen only as a reflector of the sun's light, and that's how this place existed, as you say, like a shadow, a dim theory on the other side of a lie, obscured behind the words on a page. But get across some hidden boundary and in amongst the words, then I think we change it by living it, the shadow becomes alive . . . as powerful as a life . . .'

'Or lives,' interrupts Jane.

'What, Jane?' says Rebecca.

'Well, we are not the only ones, you know! You make me really angry, the way you are both talking . . . I saw the mountains grow out of the plain and the hills form, and they didn't do it on their own . . . or because we are here. They were created out of a past and a lot of terrible pain. OK, we can give the landscape colours now, and names . . . but you are trying to make out that there isn't really a past, a past here. You come here too . . . too flippantly, like holiday makers, "Oh, we have discovered another world, how convenient, how nice". . . It isn't like that all!'

Silence.

'Sorry,' says Jane after a long pause. Then she gets up and goes away down the slope to the crack, the cat trotting behind her.

Jane beside the Crack

Jane walks off into a curtain of reeds and heat beside the crack. Detached from the others. For a while she is conscious of little more than the sensation in the soles of her feet as her sandals press into the earth of the path, satisfying . . . slightly squishy and cool. The reeds reach up on either side to her shoulders; as she parts them with her hands, they rustle, giving off a dry smell. Ahead of her, the path, winding up and down along the bank, resolves itself into a line wavering through the heat, indicating a notion of search. Gradually, the point of that search; to find a cool place under the sky which will be of no significance to anyone but herself, becomes clear in Jane's mind. Every now and again, as she hurries on, she peers out, over the tops of the reeds, across the plain at the purple mountains; the sense of distance and freedom gained from these glances stengthening her stride. At the crest of a hillock she stops. A thrill of excitement is followed by a surge of longing which spirits her, almost out of her body, to the mountains. It feels dramatic.

'Perhaps, one day, we will go climbing mountains!' she says to the cat, picking her up to show her the view, but the cat seems unimpressed.

Towards evening. They continue to make their way upstream. To their left the heavy sun mellows, waiting to fall into the lap of the land. There is a bend in the liquid course of the crack, and the path ahead sinks down into a bay held in the crook of the curve. Jane and the cat wander out of the frail reeds on to the stony shore.

The shape of the bay has condensed the sound of the flowing liquid into the air to produce an element of ringing heat, which is rising slowly. Stones, pale and uniform in shape like the caps of mushrooms, are set in the bed of the shore, glinting as water drains under them in curling veins to the crack. As they sit on the shore watching the lazy swing of the flow of the liquid, Jane feels amongst the stones at her side, selecting them without looking at them, taking them up, enjoying their smoothly rounded weight in her hands and letting them drop, one by one. Imperceptibly, her full attention is drawn down, stone by stone, and contained with them in the palm of her hand. Rubbing the surface of each stone round and round with her fingertips, she cocoons it with questions about its quality: its bleached colour? its warmth on top and coolness underneath? its age? its origin? its smell? . . . and the stones she holds surrender their characteristics to something else . . . a stony silence, a stone-age person, a stone-grey eye. Soon they are all wrapped up in ribbons of association, and she can no longer simply let them fall. She places them back down carefully. Newly wrapped in their bundles of emotion, they seem absurdly fragile and liable to be hurt, like people.

'Stones can be jolly,' declares Jane, giving the little pile she has constructed beside her a shove. The game is over. Stones roll jingling out of their imposed cocoons, and her attention is reclaimed by the movement of the liquid flowing out of the cove, and away . . . as the plain, like a magnificently colourful wing, extends fully, tilting into the light before turning to soar slowly towards the night. In the west the sun decides to fall.

Sometime later, something touches Jane from behind; a shadow. For at precisely the same moment in which the sun commenced its descent, blue shadow which had been gathering secretly around the knees of the mountains, began to journey across the plain. As it grew stealthily across the space, the blue shadow absorbed into itself other smaller shadows, the shadows of the hills and the trees, until it flowered around the fringes of the little bay where the woman in the pale dressing-gown sat. Here it claimed the shadows of the stones and then the stones themselves, the shadow of the cat and then the cat and, when Jane's shadow has melted into it, it touches her on the back of her neck. Jane feels the change but does not move as the shadow passes over her and glides away with the crack to the sea. The air in the cove begins to cool and relaxes as if it were growing old peacefully.

'Everything is deepening,' says Jane. The cat twitches, then departs abruptly into the undergrowth. Silence.

And then a sound; a quick splash, as something from the mist on the other side drops from the farther bank into the seam of the crack. The sound is produced by a small creature which has been weaving its way through the blank distance of the beyond like a needle trailing a long, long journey on a thread.

. . .

'But travelling from where?' The wistful voice of an unknown reader touches into the silence in the boat. The story stops. I put down my writing pad. The furniture in the room strikes me as being too still and oddly flat.

I don't know, I reply.

'And for how long?' creeps the whisper round the room.

As long as . . . I don't know, it has been moving from the beginning, I suppose . . . and now it slithers out . . .

'Out from where?' the initial question is repeated gently.

Out of the vegetation on the other side of the crack; reeds and rushes like this side . . . I am talking desperately at the empty visitor's chair.

'A reflection, then? Is the other side a reflection of this?'

Well, yes . . . it could be . . . but I can only glimpse the trace of a path and a few leaves . . . because . . . because of the mist over there, I finish tamely. But does it matter that I cannot see beyond the wall of mist? I stand up, but finding I have not the will to leave the room, I walk my words across the floor to the window.

You see, trying to look across to the other side is like trying to penetrate a sea of sleep or into what you are thinking . . . and when it comes to the beyond and beyond the beyond, I don't know, I don't know! I stand at the window for a long time, watching a gloomy evening washing up along the Thames. The boat is a floating body rubbing grimly against the concrete wharf. Inside, my chair and the empty visitor's chair regard each other vacantly. Whether you, the unknown reader, the new and wistful voice, are with me still, I cannot tell. Perhaps Mr Smith-god is, at this moment, leading you away like a lonely child along the towpath into the twilight.

I do not know which pale dream to follow: voices, visions, reeds tremble at the edge of the mist and evaporate. Silence. And then a splash, as the echoes are pulled together in a thread after the old woman's needle looping cleanly into the cloth.

. . .

Jane hears the splash from the other side of the crack and catches a glimpse of colour. A vivid dart of black and emerald green slips into the gleam of the surface of the liquid which is swirling gently under the heavy shadow. When the sound and the echoes, the flash of colour and the slight disturbance on the liquid surface have gone, the head and the tip of the back of the creature which has produced them appears suddenly towards the middle of the flow. It does not swim but allows itself to be borne swiftly like a twig across the crack, where a tiny ebb delivers it up on to the pebbles of the shore. It lies still in a limp wet arc; the ebb retreats and flows on towards the sea. The creature is alive, just alive, exhausted and throbbing. Sitting concealed in blue shadow, Jane distinguishes the body of the throbbing thing to be a snake. There is a black V-shaped mark on the neck, the shining body is green, tinged with purple. It is a snake with a yellow eye, a golden eye, which blinks.

A pause; a black tongue quivers at the creature's mouth, and slowly, it lifts its heavy head, stretches its neck round through the air . . . and slumps down.

'If I move I will frighten it.'

Again the head is raised, and the golden eye in the side of the head recognises a human shape perching in the gloom; aware that it does not occupy the space alone, its body shudders.

'Who is the intruder?' whispers Jane. 'Which one of us?'

A spasm of energy ripples through its body under the skin. The body moves; a twitch; then, drawing its energy together, it begins to heave itself up the beach over the stones, slowly.

'Painfully slowly,' thinks Jane, watching. She does not question the fact that the snake is intentionally inching towards her, neither does it occur to her to be frightened. Then, she sees that the skin on the snake's back is severed by a deep slash, a raw and purple wound.

102

Behind them the sun holds steady for a moment in a dip between the mountains; it shrinks away. At the distant edge of the plain, the tips of the blue shadow touch the edge of the sea.

When the snake reaches Jane it collapses into a broken coil at her feet. At length, her hand ventures out from the shadows, and, tentatively, she touches the creature on the back of the neck. The tongue flickers, the hand draws back, the body is cold. Then Jane leans forward and, quickly, with both hands, she scoops the injured creature up and into her lap. It lies there, heavy, cold, with its eyes open, in the folds of her dressing-gown. Her hair falls around her face as she bends her head and shoulders over the snake and strokes it. Occasionally, the snake lifts its head in response to the stroking, but the rest of its body remains motionless.

'You are old,' says Jane to the snake. She stops stroking it and sits quite still, as if she were waiting for it to reply . . . it does not. The only sounds to be heard in the bay are made by the liquid lapping on the shore and the wind combing dry foam through the reeds.

Slowly, the sky hardens into black, the stars come out, and, finally, the slither of a new moon rises over the mountains. The liquid in the crack sparkles on softly. Every now and again the snake stirs and looks up at Jane. It is not frightened, but, beyond this, Jane is unable to interpret the meaning in its gaze.

'What is it?' she asks. There is silence.

The woman and the creature sit in the shiny stillness for many hours. Where did the snake come from? Why did it come? Who had mutilated it so? The questions appear and are extinguished quietly by the dark. Gradually the questions cease. Jane's mind becomes cool and open under the expanse of black sky. The moonlight strengthens, and, as their slow breathing mingles towards sleep, Jane knows that she has met the creature before; in another place . . . on a high green hill in the wind.

The hours pass. Sometimes Jane tumbles awake on to the pebbles on the shore and sings to the snake. At dawn, the creature give a little shudder and dies.

When light begins to stretch with confidence across the plain and the dawn chorus is under way, Jane carefully carries the dead snake into the reeds and lays it down. The cat is waiting for her at the end of the beach. Then the woman and the cat leave the place and return, in the early morning along the damp path to the tree . . . to Helen and Rebecca.

. . .

Jane arrives back at the tree. There is no one there. Hot and tired, she doggedly climbs the green mound to the foot of the tree. She sits down on the grass, leans back against the trunk and shuts her eyes. When she opens them, she sees Helen and Rebecca walking towards her across a field, they are talking to one another. Rebecca waves.

'Look what we have found,' shouts Rebecca. 'Millions of them on a tree . . . just behind that hill.'

They have reached her, and Rebecca is handing her a red apple. Jane bites into the apple; she is very hungry.

'Are you OK?' asks Helen.

'Yes, fine,' says Jane, taking a huge chunk out of a second apple offered to her by Rebecca.

'Because we were a bit worried,' says Helen.

'No, I'm alright. I just wanted to be on my own for a while, that's all.' Helen puts her arm around her and gives her a hug.

'Look, it's no good . . .' says Helen, after a pause, her hand still on Jane's shoulder, 'we can't survive on apples.'

'Well, I'm not going hunting!' says Rebecca, imagining the three of them charging across the plain, pursuing wild deer into the sunset. She laughs.

'It's not funny.' Helen is getting hot and annoyed.

'Yes it is,' says Rebecca, 'it's all so . . . I don't know . . . predictable, somehow. Hang on tight! I can see a happy ending just around the corner! We are bound to find berries or roots of some sort at least . . . I think it is going to be all right, anyway,' she adds.

'There are two possibilities,' says Jane, 'We could go back to . . . to wherever . . .' she falters, 'or we can stay. If we stay then we have to eat, we have to *do* something!'

As the three women sit staring vaguely out at the landscape, the odd gust of wind, hurrying little bands of colour over the earth, pushes their hair out behind them; the morning sun spins light into their faces, giving them the appearance of being very bold and fearless. Helen leans back and follows the spiralling branches of the tree, leading their leaves up into the sky. She rolls over:

'I think we should go to the sea,' she says.

SECTION 13
Lilac

Saturday morning creeps along the streets between long rows of terraced houses. The rows of houses, made of dull red brick, are owned by the council; they were built shortly after the war, solid but rather shabby now. A milk float clatters round a bend, stops and clatters on, there is the occasional dog's bark, the cry of a child, but for the most part the streets are still silent. The curtains downstairs in the house on the corner of Stevenson Avenue are tugged open.

'See you later, love,' shouts her husband John, from the hall.

'OK, love,' replies Elsie.

The front door is slammed shut. Elsie stands at the window, watching John in his green overalls, whistling down the path. Bright sunlight in the cool living-room shows her a thin layer of dust on the glass cabinet and then another layer on the mantelpiece. How could all this dust have collected since Wednesday?

Instead of going into the kitchen to fetch the duster and the polish, she sits down in the armchair and observes dust falling steadily through the air on to the carpet. Beside her is a pile of ironing. In the kitchen there are already two egg-stained breakfast plates beside the sink. Upstairs, Diane and Peter are still asleep after a late night at the disco, waiting to be woken up with a cup of tea.

Elsie lights a cigarette and blows smoke out into the room, disturbing the dust in the air, forcing it for a moment to float up rather than down. The sunlight meanders lazily across the flat faces of the framed photographs on the mantelpiece and glows in abstract shapes on the orange and purple flowered carpet. The disturbed dust in the air swings down and continues to fall with delicate familiarity around her pale figure; figure in a quilted housecoat,

106

poised in the black imitation leather armchair. She feels alone, and the familiarity of the dust – not just the dust . . . the whole situation bores her to the point of annoyance. Always there is dust, little speckles of dust cascading down on her. Dust which sparkles and turns to dirt. And, as usual, she feels impelled to busy herself with the specks of dust . . . and thus her life is spent amongst the dust, ordering it like a tiny insect, building it into piles, hiding it away in bags, cupboards, dustbins. True, she isn't really alone . . . just one of many. However, this reminding herself that her position is not unusual does not make it any better or any worse . . . she still feels solitary. Is the world really rather empty, and is her life really that meaningless? Yes, Elsie supposes that it is.

'Trouble is, I haven't got any choice,' she says to herself. How many times has she reeled off this same response to these particular thoughts? 'If I don't do it, who will?' she says, allowing the response to continue its tedious refrain.

'But it would be so nice to say no for once . . . to just let the dust fall here and to go away somewhere else.' This idea, which also occurs to her frequently, is dismissed, as usual, as being ridiculous. She stubs out her cigarette in the clean, glass ashtray beside here. As she pulls herself up from the armchair, her feet reach automatically into her pink fluffy slippers on the floor. She goes into the kitchen.

The sound of activity, cupboard doors being clicked open and shut, is to be heard from the kitchen. The living-room remains flat and abandoned. Not that it makes any difference to the living-room, of course, whether Elsie is in it or not; it is prepared to wait with its walls, one purple, one black, one purple, one black, stretching inanely around the dust-laden cube of air, and the heavy glass lampshade, suspended from the white square of the ceiling, hovering over the orange and purple splotchy flowers on the carpet. The splotchy flowers at the edges of the carpet have been snipped through, so that the carpet fits exactly into the square of the floor. A tiny spider starts out from beneath a table supporting the television set in the corner and makes a dash across the carpet, disappearing under the armchair.

Elsie comes back with a mauve and white disposable cleaning

cloth and a gleaming can of spray polish. She proceeds to move all the cool glass ornaments on top of the glass cabinet to one side and squirts polish on to the surface. The polish froths over the surface, emitting a sickly smell. Elsie smears it into the glass until it disappears, moves the ornaments on to the clean area and repeats the action. When she has restored all the ornaments to their original positions, she places the little silver trophy which Peter won for the high jump in the centre. She crosses the room and follows the same procedure for the mantelpiece, shifting the photographs from one side to the other and back. Then she goes to the radio, is about to switch it on and stops . . . that would wake the kids up. On her way back to the kitchen, she kicks off her slippers under the sofa, one after the other, her hands clinging on to the can of spray polish, as if that would help her balance . . . plonk, plonk, the slippers are left to regard each other with their soft pink toes.

In the kitchen, Elsie returns the polish and the disposable cloth to the middle shelf in the cupboard by the door. She pushes up the sleeves of her housecoat and takes off her watch. She turns on the tap and dips her hands idly into the sink, where they alight on a cup.

Mrs Thompson, hurrying down the alley which runs along the back gardens on her way to the shops, observes Elsie looking out of her kitchen window. Mrs Thompson waves to Elsie and wonders if she has time to drop in for a cup of tea, but, receiving no response to her wave, she hurries on to the shops.

Elsie continues to stare out of her window at her lilac tree at the end of the garden. 'Buds! Yes, the buds are there, the buds are there amongst the leaves.'

She raises her hand, forgetting that she is holding the cup, the cup knocks against the tap and breaks in two. Elsie places the two halves of the broken cup carefully on the draining board beside the dirty breakfast plates and turns off the tap. The sink is about to overflow. She reaches into the water and pulls out the plug; the water gurgles down the plughole, and Elsie begins to sing. She sings as she fetches the bread from the larder and spreads butter over a quantity of white slices. She sings as she cuts the cheese and places it on the bread with a leaf of lettuce and a piece of tomato on each, positioning another slice of bread on top. She cuts the sandwiches through the middle and bundles them up in tin foil . . . they lie in a neat row of little packages on the formica table top. The song finishes.

Elsie unhooks the string shopping bag from the nail inside the cupboard and stuffs the sandwiches into it, along with two bars of chocolate from the kitchen drawer. She throws her housecoat off on to the chair, shoves on her shoes, grabs her coat in one hand and the string bag in the other and leaves the kitchen via the back door.

As the spider scuttles back across the carpet to the television, Elsie's son Peter walks into the living-room in his dressing-gown and blinks. 'Mum,' he shouts. The living-room is full of sunlight in which specks of dust are falling softly. Peter goes into the kitchen. 'Mum?' he says. Beneath the window he sees a broken cup on the draining board.

. . .

It's midday and I have just returned from the shops with some vegetables, milk and the newspaper. After several days of heat and April sunshine, the sky has collapsed out over us and set in a greyish pallor as thick and sickly as old cream. It is colder. A fine wind scrapes across the dull surface of the wide river and the water in my backwater is slapping unevenly against the side of the boat. The trees across the river are now all the same shade of green. They stand in a drab row, unexuberant and demure, as if the vitalising spirit had withdrawn from their leaves, as if after the struggle to establish spring, they were bored with growing and were fed up with being tugged about by the wind. The odd swallow whips a keen line from one point to another, flying fast and low like a bird in a cage. The lilac blossoms in the white vase beside me on the table have flopped their heavy heads on top of one another; they perform their gentle death expiring mauve fragrance. I see . . .

I see three women and a cat walking through a wavering field of summer grass and summer flowers, away from the crack in the direction of the sea. The sky is high and blue; the sun is in the sky. I can see, from the way they halt and then move on again, that they are engrossed in conversation. The woman on the left of the trio, in blue jeans and blue jumper, who pauses and stoops to examine something in the grass beside the path, is Helen. She jumps up with the point of a yellow flower in her hand and runs after the others. Now they stop and consider the flower. Rebecca crouches over the foliage on her side of the path, Helen and Jane stand beside here, looking down also. Rebecca gets up and they move away. Stopping and starting, sometimes running a little distance into the field and bounding back to the path; women walking on through the bright morning field, field of flowers and shimmering glory. The path, at the end of the field, winds around the skirts of two small hills, the women round the bend of the first hill, followed by the cat. They disappear.

THE END

. . .

'What do you mean, the end?' The words of the unknown reader drift into the boat from an obscure opening in the long, grey tunnel afternoon. I pick up my pen again.

OK. There are two green hills (I roll the words across the page and stop to doodle around them) . . . and miles and miles of fields and woods (the pen trails on) . . . and more hills and a few clouds, and it's getting hotter, and the smell of the sea brings excitement welling up . . .

'Come on, what's around the first corner?' The voice slips away. Silence.

'What about a gate?' prompts another woman's voice, a familiar voice.

Why not? Yes, there is a gate (I mark it down carefully . . . A gate).

'And beyond the gate is a little muddy path leading into another field, a field full of buttercups, because they are your favourite . . .' adds yet another woman's voice, also familiar.

'And this buttercup field has a hedge round it,' (a hedge . . .) 'and at the far end there is a row of trees and a stream.' Familiar voice number three. (I scribble in the stream and the line of trees, which grow into woods . . . bluebell woods, with secret glades and dells . . . I like secret glades and dells . . . and so, picking up the thread of the narrative, I continue:)

110

Rounding the bend, the three women come to a gate, which they open; then they follow the muddy path through the golden buttercup field, walking in single file until they come to another gate . . . No, I can't have another gate.

'Well, it looks like a gate to me!' announces the first familiar voice. I look up and peer out of my window at the river which floats on, blankly, seductively, on and on, through the dull afternoon. Perhaps there was a gate once, but there isn't one anymore . . . no, I definitely can't have another gate (then pen to paper: new paragraph:)

The women walk out of the field through a space where there was, there might be, there once had been, a gate, used in the past, by women for . . . (The pen hovers, scratching in the air for something women did in the past with gates . . . and drops back to the page . . . for swinging on when they were children, it inscribes.)

'But we still do that!' shouts Rebecca, climbing on to the imaginary gate which is a gate. The three women are laughing at me! This makes me rather cross. I feel like a mother whose children have got out of control.

'We know,' says Helen, turning in front of the gate, hands on hips. 'We can tell you anything and you will believe it!'

But I was beginning to see the wood . . .

'See what I mean!' says Helen.

But I don't believe just anything . . . anyway, you are lucky you are not in a book, being written by some man, that's all I can say! Just imagine what would become of you when entering the bluebell wood . . . Sometimes I think I am too humble about writing this; what with trying to accommodate the demands of this elusive unknown reader and then having to work out where you have got to and build you up and try and make you all 'convincing' . . . and to add to that, I'm continually under attack from Smith-god and Jones!

'So are we,' says Jane, playing with the cat. 'I think the trouble is that you want to be here as well.'

Well, I am, aren't I? Who are you talking to if I am not there? The sky?

'But you are sitting in a houseboat,' says Rebecca.

Pause . . . Can you see me, then?

'Of course we can bloody see you!' she says.

I look round the dim room, slowly . . . just now, when I was writing about the field and the gate, I could see them out on the plain, but I heard their voices inside the boat . . . there is no one here, except my cat asleep on the bed in a tight ball.

You never told me you could see me . . .

'It isn't very often,' says Jane. 'It wasn't until Helen told us that we are characters in a book . . . anyway, why don't you walk out here yourself?'

Because . . . I would like to . . . I would like to chuck my pen in the river and wander off, but I can't because the story doesn't move if I do that.

'I don't see how you can say that if you aren't here!' says Helen. OK, but what about the other voice, the shadow voice of the unknown reader who is always offering me the pen and disappearing?

'Yes,' says Rebecca. 'You see . . .' she turns to Helen; they jump down from the gate and carry on towards the wood, talking.

Jane, Jane! I shout to the woman in the dressing-gown leaning against the gate. Jane, I want to give you a hug, I want you to give me . . . Then Jane opens the gate and she and the cat walk through; I see her turn to close it behind them. Yellow field spins away.

Six-thirty, lilac twilight sags down inside the boat. On my way to the kitchen to make tea, I notice that someone has switched on the light out in the yard.

. . .

The women reach the edge of the field and pass, one behind the other, under the green cover of the wood.

In the wood the slender trunks of trees stretch up through trembling patterns of new growth. High in their branches birdsong ripples, splashing downwards between softer shafts of light. And the floor spreads and spreads and melts in pools of bluebells and thin areas of bright green bladed grass. As the women tramp amongst the trees, following a little windy path, dead sticks crunch and snap loudly under their feet. This sound rushes with other sounds, the calls of the birds and the rustling of the leaves, towards the still womb of the wood. Silence echoes back. Senses are heightened, they divide . . . sound and silence. Sounds repeat, but always from a different, invisible point, as small life stirs or breaks and is washed over by the repetition of silence. Then, like the notes in a song, the path separates out of itself. Smaller paths lead off into pools of colour, tranquil patches of sunlight, intimate hollows of decay. Along them the women move like shadows, weaving in and out of the straight trunks of trees and twirling brambles, until they can no longer see each other and are connected only by threads of sound.

Each woman walks on her own curving path into the network of growth; and to each it seems that she is sinking alone through floating patches of mauve time into the smell of the earth and down, into the moisture of the roots and down, her body reducing steadily into its own tight core . . . to be recalled by the sound of a twig snapping or the slant of a ray of sunlight upon a petal of fungus, to move on, weaving her way like a pale shoot up to where green is piled on green, and the air softly transfuses clarity and is light.

The women on paths pass and repass, alerting each other with glimpses of bright clothing flashing into shadow, meeting in a speckle of sound. Sometimes they are far, far out, riding on waves through qualities of silence: silence in light, silence in shadow, to the birth of silence. Separately, they return with silence to particular points in the wood, where they listen and smell and touch and see. As now, it is Rebecca who discovers an area, clear except for a single tree, and steps forward. She rests with her head against the trunk, her ear pressed to the crust of bark, breathless, dizzy and glad.

The shadows of the women twist on deeper and darker, leaving behind the places where spaces of bluebells reflect the sky, until even the fine threads of light penetrating the foliage slowly die out like the last drips of rain; the wood is all shaking shadow, and the occasional sound merely an echo from somewhere else which fears to follow. And here, in the thickest depths, the women meet beside a small dark pool, soggy with moss, glowing emerald from a source below the earth. Here, they sit in a concentrated circle, bodies leaning gently forward, hair hanging down. And here, their strengths touch, and knowledge is reborn, quietly, without fuss, emerald gift emerging, emerging out of purple darkness.

. . .

The black cat strolls out of the bushes into the sunshine and leaps easily on to the wooden fence which marks the boundary on the farther side of the wood. She settles her body neatly on to the small circular top of a post, considers the distance and waits, ears pointing up, tail dangling down. Soon the sound of voices, calling encouragingly to one another in the trees behind her, reaches her ears, causing them to twitch.

'I think we are almost there!'

'Come on, Jane, not much farther now!'

A wave of commotion, produced by branches being pushed aside and dead sticks cracking, arises in the undergrowth and subsides suddenly, as Rebecca, Helen and Jane scramble out of the brambles and climb on to the fence.

They are exhausted. The sun flings heat down on to their heads, on to their hands clasping the rail of the fence. Ahead, a mustard field hums into the silence of green hills, and from beyond the hills a smell drifts back to them: the smell of the sea.

The little path skirting the woods turns to run beside the fence where the women are sitting. Along the path walks a figure in a summer dress, carrying a shopping bag in one hand and a raincoat in the other. It is Jane who notices Elsie first; quickly she drops from the fence and goes to meet her.

SECTION 14
Ruby's Story

April morning. The blossom squeezes out and sticks on
to the stiff branches of the cherry tree in little processions of quick
shrill kisses . . . kiss, kiss, kiss.

'Look, how delightful the tree is!' says her mother, standing
beside her at the window. 'Look how complete it is!' The blossom
has smothered its naked black form.

Ruby turns away from the window and goes to sit down at the
dressing-table. There, before her, her head and shoulders are
encased by the frame of the mirror. Behind her, also encased, she
can see her white iron bed with its pretty duvet thrown back as she
had left it, and her teddy bear, given to her by her father when she
was a child, lying with its back to her and gazing at the pretty
wallpaper, which is sprinkled with tiny flowers to match the duvet.

'All right, dear?' Her mother pats her shoulder. She stands
behind her daughter and addresses her reflection in the mirror. The
reflection smiles graciously, and the older woman leaves the room.

'My mother does not love me,' says Ruby to her reflection, and the
reflection smiles again. This is the first time it happens . . . a jolt.
Inside, she feels herself being swung off into a black tunnel, a tunnel
in the underground . . . then light; a station, another day, another
chance . . . and into the mirror sweeps her mother again, bearing
a cup of coffee. 'She is idiotic,' whispers Ruby to her reflection.

'There, it will be all right, dear.' Her mother is tired. She pats the
cotton material of the nightie which covers her daughter's shoulder
and, continuing to pat, shoots a glance at the cherry tree, white
blossom piled up on its branches. 'Charming,' she says and leaves
the room hastily, remembering at the last moment to bring the door
to, carefully, as if she were securing an invisible lock.

Ruby places the coffee cup in the corner of the reflection and practises. She practises pushing the smile up and across the face looking at her, rearranging it.

'There, it'll be all right, dear . . . Look at the tree, how complete it is!' echo the words, and deep inside she is flung back on course in the rattling train. On course, off course . . . she isn't sure. Beneath the dressing-table her hands tighten their grasp on the wooden seat of the chair. The individual buds at the tips of the branches sway slightly in the wind; soon it will be their turn to burst open into the sunshine in the garden.

The door opens once more. Ruby does not move. She sits before the mirror, watching her mother smooth out the bottom sheet on the bed and take hold of the duvet; with a swift, deliberate flap, her bed is sealed off from her forever. No ceremony. The teddy bear is propped against the blue and white flowery wall and slips down, feet in the air, eyes fixed on the ceiling. The door closes gently.

Ruby makes herself busy. She selects a tube from the row of pots and tubes at the foot of the mirror. Slowly, she squeezes a large, cold white blob on to her finger, blob with a little peak. Briskly, automatically, dab, dab, dab . . . she taps her face with her finger. She stares closely into the mirror. The blobs make her face look silly. She turns to share the joke with the teddy bear; he continues to gaze at the ceiling. Angry, she works the cream into her skin, rubbing the flesh hard, deep into the pores. Again she practises the smile.

At intervals the garden gate clicks open and shut. At intervals the bedroom door opens and closes. Dumb mouths without words. And, at intervals, a single blossom pops out, its courage unnoticed, into the air.

Now, behind her face in the mirror, she observes her mother at work, burying the bed under armfuls of crisp white clothing. The white pile grows rapidly, becoming frillier and frillier. Her mother pauses, raising her hand to her brow; something forgotten . . . and exits. Quietly, Ruby applies colour to her face, pale peaches and cream to go with her hair, and practises. The smile becomes easier as the layers on her face thicken. Once, finger poised in mid air above a pot, she looks up too early, before the smile has been hoisted, and catches a glimpse of . . . such emptiness! A great, glaring emptiness, sad as a lonely hill. Quickly, she bobs her head down and dips her finger into a pot of blue powder. When she ventures to look up again, her fingertip blued in readiness to apply shadow to her eyes, the reflection flaps a smile reassuring, like a flag, back at her. A flag raised by a solemn procession of men in robes on the lonely hill. 'It'll be all right,' it flaps.

Ruby gets up. When her mother returns, she finds her daughter standing in front of the mirror in her wedding dress.

'Oh Ruby . . . Ruby!' she exclaims. 'Come downstairs now, my darling, and see your flowers; they arrived just a few minutes ago.' She looks out of the window. 'A blackbird!'

They withdraw from the room, the door closes. A single blossom unfolds into delicate fullness on a branch outside; the blackbird pierces it with his orange beak, then throws back his head in song. The teddy bear continues to stare at the ceiling, blankly.

When Ruby enters the sitting-room her father rises from the sofa to look at her . . . she smiles.

. . .

Sunlight paddles up the still suburban street. Buildings dip their shadows into the pavement, people wander through; it is midday. Every now and again, when there happen to be no cars on the road, there is a hint of the eternal, a calm so deep that the people walking along the paths are almost aware of it. Aware, as they step between the shadows, of layers of time: now present but now future, now past. And out of the past, it seems almost, from over the top of the hill, between the grocer's and the chemist's, creeps a procession, or rather the visible part of a procession which is always there, though often invisible, and people take note and watch. Three black cars, the first with ribbons tied to the bonnet. When the first car slows up beside the passers-by at the traffic lights, they see inside a woman's face beneath a netted veil. Flat. Her eyes stare into their own reflection trapped in the supermarket window, her mouth flickers. The traffic lights change to green; the procession whirls on around the corner.

. . .

The white bride flutters along the path in the sunlight like a petal on a current of air and is sucked into the church porch. The porch is cold and smells of death. The smell seizes her by the throat. Her grey-clad father senses her shudder.

'It'll be all right.' He strokes her hand sentimentally as if to brush off her fear. She clings tightly on to her father's arm and hoists her smile. Her father leads her to the inner doorway and propels her through. Inside, penned people shuffle in their stalls and are quiet. High in a loft a figure in black jabs at the organ, blithely. Again Ruby feels the grasping sensation at her throat. The sound of the organ is strident, aggressive: 'Stab, stab the bride!' It drags her up the aisle between rows of gaping faces. At the foot of the steps, with his back to her, a man is waiting; his friend at his side has one hand in his jacket pocket. And facing them, on the steps, is Mr Smith-god in long robes. He extends a loose-sleeved arm in welcome, drawing her towards him with the ease of one landing an insignificant fish. Nearing the end of a dark tunnel, Ruby turns her head to one side; her mother will not look at her; she is gazing straight ahead at the altar from under her new hat, her lip is trembling. The procession and the sound from the organ come to an abrupt halt, jolting into a hefty weight of silence. Then Mr Smith-god raises his voice: 'Dearly Beloved, we are gathered together . . .'

Ruby hears few of the words. She clutches her flowers, the words chase round and round her neck, she is spinning in a tunnel . . . dark. Light, the man beside her is lifting her hand, then dark, and she is stranded on a lonely hill on which a bonfire has been built. Hands are tying her to a stake.

'Psalm twenty-three.' They are chanting:

'The Lord is my shepherd,
I shall not want.
He maketh me down to lie . . .'

During this, Mr Smith-god, invigorated by the music, tramps around in a little male dance, showing off the swish of his robes.

'In pastures green . . .'

Above the altar, glass of beautiful colours, light beyond, and in the colours swims a gentle face. For a moment she sees a dreamy hope rising around the face in the shape of gardens, fountains, valleys green. Ruby smiles at the face.

'Yea, though I walk in death's dark vale . . .'

Then quiet; the face fades as the sun outside is cuddled into a cloud. In the quiet the shrill cry of a blackbird on a tree in the graveyard penetrates her soul.

'Ahem,' coughs Mr Smith-god. The faces in the pews are recalled from where they have been . . . perhaps on a hillside in the dark, watching a torch begin to burn.

'Jonathan was a bachelor gay,' sings out Mr Smith-god to the assembly. He beams brightly at the man next to her. 'And Ruby . . .' he pauses. She feels the load of his 'understanding' leaning on top of her like an elbow; he lowers his voice as if to utter a dirty word . . . 'a spinster'. Silence. She offers him the quiver of a smile requested by this sad pause. He continues with the happy ending of the tale. 'But now they are one, united forever in the eyes of . . .'

The final hymn springs up like flames around her feet and she is being wafted down the tunnel to the door. Halfway down the tunnel, she notices that, somewhere in the middle of it all, someone has slipped a ring on to her finger.

. . .

Emerging from the church porch, Ruby blinks in the sunlight and, becoming aware of the faces surrounding her in a semicircle, blinks again. She offers them her smile and is greeted by a storm of noise; it seems to please them.

Then, they arrange themselves in little lines either side of her. The photographer backs into the branches of the pink cherry tree, snapping the twigs; as petals fall, he pushes the button on the camera . . . click. High on the spire a blackbird thrusts up a song like a trumpeter. Ruby smiles.

. . .

119

A small row of people, well-dressed and stationary, curves like a branch into the drafty church hall. Ruby stands at its tip, trapped in white net. Past them file the guests. Ruby feels their faces bend, one by one, towards her. Secret, sickly smells accompany the faces which peer then peck or kiss her cheek. Sometimes the arm of a black suit slides around her waist, dabbling its fingers playfully into the netting at the back of her garment. At the same time the mouth in the face above the suit is chattering excitedly, diverting attention, so that no one but he and Ruby will know about the fingers lingering in the material at the base of her spine. How pleased they all are . . . 'We are so pleased,' they whine.

They sit around a rectangle of tables in the vast church hall. The square at the centre of the rectangle is empty. Perched at the top table, Ruby sits sipping champagne, turning the glass in her hand, turning the food on her plate. She is silent and smiling. An embarrassed murmur settles around the tables, punctuated by the tinkling clatter of knives and forks. Occasionally, a child shouts or someone drops a knife on the floor, slicing the noise apart, and the murmur of voices retreats to a corner. A pause, and then the guests bend their heads and gratefully remember what they were saying or what they were about to say, and the murmur rises once more and settles. Then silence, and one of the men at her table is standing up; he stumbles through a series of sounds and gestures. They all clap their hands. Ruby watches. She dips her finger into the yellow champagne in her glass, making a space for a bubble to rise . . . Someone is anxiously pinching her leg under the table. 'Ruby, stop that!' her mother whispers.

When Ruby looks up again, she is surprised to see activity. The empty square is flooding outwards. Tables, chairs and people are deposited at the walls. The light has changed; the hall has become a place of shadows, dim except for the bright points of cigarettes . . . which softly smoke and add smoke to the gloom. The stiff, steady murmur has dissolved, and detached pockets of sound rise up: whispers, shrieks, circles trembling on the verge of laughter. The groups of people remind her of birds gathered in a chilly cave. Her table is not moved; she remains where she is, perched behind it, smiling bravely. Individual birds, feathers slightly battered, swim towards her across the space to peck at her cheek, or sometimes it is two who come together.

Suddenly, from a corner, music crashes into the space and fills it. Heads poke up, startled for a moment, then back down. As Ruby watches, the little groups seem to be retreating from her, slowly washing away. 'It's time to go,' he says, taking her arm.

'Oh.' It is all she can reply.

Somehow, she allows herself to be supported on to her feet. Scuffling in the room, she suffers herself to be pecked at again by one of the birds.

'Mother!' she cries, and louder, 'Mother!'

'It'll be all right, dear,' says her mother, inclining her head away from Ruby towards the door.

On top of the next burst of music the bride floats awkwardly out of the mouth of the hall . . . and away to sea.

'Charming,' her mother's voice trembles, 'I'll remember this day . . . a day to remember.'

That was a long time ago.

Ruby sits on a lily leaf revolving slowly through the darkness and the light. Locked in silence, smiling.

Elsie is Walking

At the far end of the boat, beyond the living-room, there is a musty room which I could not use in the winter because of the cold and the damp. Some friends of my parents have given me an elegant old desk with finely shaped legs and two thin drawers. I have cleaned out the room, polished the desk and positioned it under the windows. The room is tiny; the walls are pale pink and peeling, grey blots of damp are spotted on the ceiling and in the corners are spiders' webs which I did not want to damage. On the floor there is a shabby Indian rug, retrieved from the rubbish dump in the yard. I have added a plant, which stands on a little round table to one side, and pinned some pictures of women and a couple of poems on the wall. Behind a heavy velvet curtain, up three wide shiny steps, desk, chair, carpet, plant . . . the room is ready; it waits.

In the mornings when I draw back the curtain from the entrance, my fingers tremble . . . task ahead. I put down my coffee cup on the desk, I slide the drawers open and closed, I reread what I have written the day before, I test pens on paper. From the windows I have a clear view across the width of the river to the trees on the other side which are now in flower. I watch the water, I gauge its pace . . . today, slow and easy. So much happens on the river; the busy pair of ducks, for instance, have had fifteen babies. They leave their nest below the bridge to swim past regularly. But as the days pass, the number of ducklings diminishes, like the nursery rhyme:

> 'Quack, quack!' says Mother Duck,
> 'Come back, come back!'
> And fourteen little ducks come back.

Sometimes the cat comes and sits on the desk; we watch together, thinking separate thoughts. Yesterday we saw a kingfisher, turquoise and orange, exquisite, rare. And each day the rhythm of the water is different; it metamorphoses before our eyes, calm, silent, chopping, tones exchanging. Rain flashes and sun pours. The sun hits the room in the early afternoon; rapidly, the room becomes very hot. I continue to sit, melting page, melting body, the boat rocks. There is a pot of nasturtiums and a pot of cornflowers up on the roof; they are my sign to the world that activity is going on down here below, now that I no longer need to light the stove and send no more signals up in smoke.

At night my dreams are vivid; I do not know if I am speeding up or slowing down. For a week I have been caught in a recurring dream . . . a circle dream in which the boat sinks. The nights are mild and clear. Before sleep I climb on to my roof and sit in my dressing-gown under the stars. I pray to the new moon which rises above the shed in the boatyard. The inhabitants of the other boats are asleep; the boats rock quietly on the water in the starlight.

I am awake in my sleep. I know that someone else is in the boat, undressing behind the curtain at the end of the bed. I feel the creek of the springs, the sag of the mattress, as a heavy body creeps under the covers beside me. I steer off, out of reach, into a dream. I am hauled back through the dark to the weight, the presence, of the body which is breathing deeply. The body stirs, and, in a low and eerie light, the fat face of Mr Smith-god looms above me. He has shaved off his beard, his cherry eyes flare chisel bright, his mouth, alert, is smiling. 'In 1966, I received a circular,' he whispers with obscure precision. He is walking the tips of his flexible fingers up my body under the bedclothes. Thick hands hang around my throat. I cry for help and he smiles. I mouth the word 'help' over and over in the dark. The process of strangulation sinks me through hours of night, years. I mouth my word . . . and make no sound. Just before it is over, I grip my thin strength together in a final effort and shout '*Help!*' the sound comes loud and I have woken myself up with my own scream. After a long time, I crawl down the bed across the soft blanket to the light and switch it on; there is no one in the boat.

I clamber up and out into the fragile moonlight on the roof. I pray to the moon. She raises me up; I grow thinly, but taller and taller, I lift into the spangle of stars. Peering down over the tops of houses, I spy him on the roof of my boat; a squat, little blob, alone and croaking in the night. For when I grow tall, Mr Smith-god goes all squashy and small, and, from up here, given the whimsical perspective of a star, I almost feel quite fond of him . . . in the way one might feel fondness, perhaps, for a fat little frog. And, maybe, I will stoop to tie a cobweb around his podgy form and trail him, hopping after me, on a silver string, as I stride off into the distance amongst the wonderful stars. Maybe.

. . .

Things happen. My friends come to visit me on the boat; I make it tidy and offer them tea. We talk. I go for bicycle rides in the afternoon. In the evenings I read women writers avidly, I watch the news on television which on occasion makes me so angry that I scream and rage about the room. Money is scarce, but sometimes I can afford to go into London on the train; I attend exhibitions, peace marches and demonstrations against the political situation in South Africa. But most of my time I spend with my cat and myself and the women out on the plain. This has all been so for quite a while now, a series of moons; the ducks have had their ducklings, the new room has opened up, the trees are green across the river, and white with horse chestnut flowers.

I sit here with the afternoon sunlight spreading on to the page, trying to recount how Elsie, carrying the little packages of food in her shopping bag, reaches the point beyond the wood where the women are sitting on the fence. I am having difficulty; she won't be forced. I try one way, then another, fixing threads together, one from here, one from out there. Elsie refuses my imposed connections; she won't, for instance, fall down a hole and pop up obligingly in the middle of the bluebell wood! And as I fail to make her do this or that, my respect for her grows, and she becomes irritated with me and her mother-provider role. She runs like a money spider over the page; I manipulate her back on to the straight lines with the point of my pen. I try to guide her from line to line, to make her trail mesh, weave in correctly with those of the women out on the plain. She will not be fitted in. Undaunted, she humps her packages around in her own direction and I fling netted cries, 'Mother, Mother!' after her. She becomes flustered, her cheeks flush under her grey perm. It is almost the smell of her which I find so attractive.

Mother smell. In the dark I pull back the covers and slide into bed, the boat heaves off into another troubled night. Through the dark many unwieldy shapes grow into the palms of hands, rising red and black before my eyes. Mother smell, sweet . . . mother, mother I see red. Mr Jones raises his scarlet sleeve, places a horn to his lips and blasts a red-coated hunting party scattering into the distance; streaks of red. They take the scent of the maternal trail, they pursue her as if she were a fox. Beside a roaring bonfire Mr Smith-god is waiting, idly pouring milk into the flames. I cry out, 'Mother, Mother do not die!'

When red flames subside into solemn darkness, father and son meet. Mr Smith-god pokes the ashes with a stick and ghosts of mothers, thin and bitter, creep out weeping across the night. Then dismal father and son console each other and together they condemn the cruel mother for all misdeeds, for war and pain; she is to blame . . . for has she not deserted them?

I climb out of the burning vessel on to my roof in the dark and sit under the moon until the boat is calm, and is now a boat floating on the river in the moonlight.

. . .

Clean morning. I watch Elsie the spider trickle a meandering path down my writing paper. Elsie. She reaches the edge of the page and, dropping to the floor, crawls off around the leg of my chair. I do nothing but sit here riding bright reflections out across the water. Slowly the morning unpeels becoming large and warm. Sometime after midday I decide to abandon the attempt to write; I stretch my arms, am about to stand up, when my attention is caught by the figure of a woman hurrying along between the trees on the other side of the river, a woman carrying a shopping bag: Elsie has crossed the bridge.

. . .

Ahead of her tall horse chestnut trees stand in quiet groups and rock their great white flowers graciously into bloom. Elsie treads into the cradle path. Before long she comes to a gap in the trees and pauses to look across the river at a motley collection of houseboats huddled on the farther side, and at one boat in particular, a big, green, oblong boat. At the end of this boat are two square windows, they look like hollow eyes. But then the sunlight, picking its way from boat to boat, touches the green boat and the windows seem to blink at her as if they were alive. 'Strange,' she says.

The river leads the path out of the trees. The air is heavy with river smells drying quickly in the heat. She is getting hot. Continuous noise buzzes rudely from the main road on the other side. She looks across at the backs of shops, working out which is which: the butcher's, the supermarket, the shoeshop . . . At the back of the shoeshop she sees a door open and a box hurled carelessly into the litter in the yard. This sight makes her smile. 'It always looks so smart from the front.'

Then, from out of the crowded rooftops behind the shoeshop, the copper spire of a church spears the sky and a single bell strikes; one o'clock, she has forgotten her watch. The sun rains indifferently on to the rooftops. There is so much noise! She can make out ragged cries, blasts from radios, the belt of a siren . . . but all the while Elsie is moving forward, away from the snatching chaos on the other side. She reaches the point where the river divides.

It is quieter. There is no one else around; she stops to rest on a wooden bench and admire the splendid new building belonging to the yachting club, which sits sedately on the wedge of green island in the middle of the river opposite. She has never been this far before, although she has read about the building in the local paper. It has little triangular flags, red, blue and white, pinned to its eaves, gaily coloured boats made out of plastic are tethered to the bank . . . a scene from a postcard or a travel brochure. A family of ducks swims past, quacking loudly. Elsie picks up her shopping bag and her raincoat and hurries on.

Soon she has left the yachting club behind; now there are large houses with patios and terraces facing her across the river. They all have immaculate lawns with paths winding carefully down to the willows at the water's edge. 'Perfect,' she thinks, but then she is wondering why she doesn't really like them. Once or twice a solitary voice washes over to her; people are calling to each other to come inside for lunch, but these cries are faint, they hardly reach her.

Elsie walks more slowly. Again the trees stand close beside one another, bushes drift into position around their trunks, so that now she can only catch the occasional glimpse of the houses beyond the sparkle of the water. The path slides on through a tunnel of foliage, patches of light glide away into the bushes. It is cooler and, at last, there is silence. Silence apart from the sound of the river flowing, dissolving the bank on the other side . . . then the trees open out once more, the water glows up golden; the other side has disappeared. Elsie is walking beside the crack.

. . .

Although the distance between Jane and Elsie, approaching one another on the path beside the bluebell wood, is not very great, it seems to both that they are taking an endless amount of time to actually reach each other. Jane smiles, Elsie grins, and the path seems to stretch them apart. Jane fidgets with the cord around the waist of her dressing-gown; she is too hot. The cat runs eagerly in front of her almost tripping her up. Elsie stops grinning and swops her shopping bag from one hand to the other. Without warning, the strain of the distance collapses and they are only a few yards apart.

'Hello,' calls Jane; she giggles. She giggles because it is all too awkward, too unreal, but her laughter causes the silence to snap. Elsie laughs as well. 'I've brought you some food,' she shouts, holding up the shopping bag.

Jane leads Elsie like a queen to where the spectators, Helen and Rebecca, are standing leaning against the fence. Helen regards Elsie thoughtfully; yes, she is familiar. 'Hello!' she says, 'I didn't expect to see you here.'

'I didn't expect to come! . . . but it's very pretty, isn't it?' replies her cleaning lady.

The four women sit at the edge of the mustard field. Elsie takes the packages of sandwiches and bars of chocolate from her shopping

127

bag and spreads them out on the grass. Apples are produced from pockets. The vision is a simple one, it crystallises, vivid before me as if from an ancient memory: the heat of the summer, the spinning yellow sun, yellow field . . . the voices and laughter of women sharing food together in the open air.

SECTION 16

Sea

It is evening when the four women reach the shingle slope beside the sea. They climb up on to the ridge and turn to face the plain, watching quietly as the heavy sun splutters down into the distant mountains, gulping colours out of the land and squirting them up into the sky in shrieking shapes: orange, purple, red. At violent speed, a flock of birds shoots black over orange and disappears. Winds with lowered heads sway out from the base of the mountains, jerking blindly round the hills, through the trees and into the women forcing back their clothes and their hair. As the glaring sky crumples in over the distance, the other side of the crack, and anything which might have been creeping or drifting about beyond, is sealed off. On this side a lonely tree stands guarding the edge like the body of a woman untouched in flames, and the crack glows strongly through the darkening land, radiating power, protecting the plain from the turbulance above.

'Bloody hell,' says Elsie. 'I've never seen a sky like that!'

'No, neither have I,' says Rebecca.

A spirit of calm is spreading in from the sea, settling the shadows, gently blowing out the spurts of birdsong. If a song strikes up again, after the calm has passed, the women can feel her patiently retracing her steps to blow again and they hear the song diminish and go out like a light. But there is anger in the sky, its colours are too bright; they growl and clash into each other, red into purple into orange, bloody. The calm spirit trails on beneath, sadly, as if she has seen too much suffering.

They stand on the windy ridge in the hem of the shadow and turn now towards the sea, which slaps and slaps against the shore, sending tiny frills of water sucking up the beach. On either side the beach flies away in a squiggly line. Ahead, the wooden shell of a small boat lies face down on the sand, hunched over as if nurturing a fugitive or a crab in the dark space under itself.

The women slither down the slope and steal towards the boat. Feet on shingle, feet on sand. They stand around it in silence, their clothes flapping in the evening breeze, the sea moaning.

'Shall we?' says Helen.

They turn the boat over, half expecting the thing which it seemed to be sheltering to scuttle away . . . but there is nothing under it, except four straight oars lying innocently, waiting. In the half light they drag the boat down the beach. It touches the flopping waves thankfully and rocks lightly on the shallow water. Hastily shoes and socks are pulled off and flung into the bottom of the boat. The women wade into the sea. Rebecca holds the boat steady, and one by one they hoist themselves up and over the side and find a place to sit: Elsie and Helen behind Rebecca and Jane.

The boat inches out from the shore. Darkness falls. For a while there is nothing but the rhythmic sound of the oars in the water and the creak of the oars turning in their sockets. Four women row through the night. Apart from each other, they can see nothing; the land has disappeared. It is cooler but they do not feel cold; they sway back and forth, back and forth, lost in the rhythm of the oars. From time to time, they look round into each other's faces, softened, just visible through the dark. They cast glances across to one another, stitching and stretching contact: Rebecca to Helen, Helen to Jane, Jane to Elsie, Elsie to Rebecca. On the flat bottom of the boat toes meet, occasionally in the air knees rub together, hands curled round the smooth handles of the oars touch and heave apart.

Separate, distinct, alive in the dark, each woman is with herself, being rocked smaller and smaller over the surface as the volume of water underneath increases, and the boat bobs higher to meet each wave and descends into the gulf behind it. When they are far, far out, the thin moon rises suddenly into the sky, like a boat, a silhouette reflection of themselves, strewing a silver sheen over the darkness above and laying down a fragile path, a vital twisting thread on the surface of the sea for the women to travel along. Another thread of light, a thinner thread, unseen by the women in the boat, is laid down also, to drift out across the surface of the dark water until it touches the hand of a lonely woman who sits on a lily leaf far, far out, revolving slowly. Then the moon lifts up, drawing the dripping threads after her high into the night sky, and Ruby, the woman who sits on the lily leaf, stares, as she turns, into her tiny reflection, dappling faintly on the surface of the vast ocean. Silence. The boat containing four women advances along its silver line through the dark.

One of the women begins to sing. Elsie sings a song which she has forgotten she knew – a lullaby which weaves around the boat in a magic chant. She sings as the four oars rustle in and out of the water; the boat rocks, and Elsie rocks against Helen beside her. On and on the boat travels under the moon arch in the sky. The path before them across the waves widens, and the ripples on the path glow out in tinges of colour like the colour at the heart of the tiny white flowers on the horse chestnut tree, or the colour in the core of the shell: the birth of mauve, pink and yellow. The boat slows down and stops.

'I'm exhausted,' says Jane. All of a sudden she remembers the cat. The cat is not with her, but somewhere else on the land, stalking through the shadows on the plain, unseen, alone.

The women rest in the tossing boat. They do not speak. For a while their particular thoughts pause together, then they separate, taking their leave to journey across the surface in different directions like travellers going home in the dark. These various thoughts concern: an abandoned easel, an empty canvas propped against the wall in a dim flat in south London; two teenage children asleep after a disco; a male student reading in bed, his head supported by his arm; and the black cat prowling on an invisible path through tall, wet grass beside the crack. The thoughts flow out in the quality of the moonlight, they reach the edges of the worlds to which they belong and wash in over the boundaries. A pale ray crosses the floor of the studio in the flat in London and seeps around the walls, so that they quiver with an iridescence, almost moist, like the inside of an organ preparing to engender life. In Elsie's house, Diane and then Peter, in their bedrooms opposite each other across the hall, discover themselves suddenly wide awake in their beds in the middle of the night; they register the moonlight and turn from one dream to another, gratefully, as they did when they were young and woke to find their mother standing in the doorway. Not far away, Philip, the student in the university residence, puts down his book, yawns, and switches off the bedside lamp. Elsewhere, the black cat pads on towards the tree through the night.

'The clarity of the moon is so different from the clarity of the sun,' thinks Rebecca, 'it has a kind of inquiring knowledge.'

Because they are no longer rowing, because their bodies are still, the women feel cool, like individual flames going out . . . cool and then cold. Now, a raw wind scrapes over the surface and jabs at the end of the boat so that it jerks awkwardly from side to side, knocking them against one another. The moon retreats silently behind a cloud. Jane gathers the collar of her dressing-gown tightly around her neck and sits huddled up inside the inadequate garment. This position flings a memory at her; like a black, wet thing jumping out of the sea, flabby. It is caught by the wind and slaps across her face, stinging . . . the old fear starts to swell. Jane hunched inside her dressing-gown, Jane lost and cold, Jane waiting for the return of a man who would not return, who slapped her in the face and left her by herself, Jane facing a blank door, a dissolving door which dissolves and dissolves in water in the dark . . . Jane . . . Jane . . .

She is distracted by a considerable amount of scrabbling on the floor of the boat; the hands of the other women are fumbling around for shoes and socks. As Jane reaches down for her sandals, the moon glides out of the grasp of the cloud and rushes a bright pulse of light along the path resting on the water. The women look up and meet the fear in each other's faces, strained and white in the moonshine.

Far across the waves, Ruby, who sits on the lily leaf, is also disturbed by the shock of light. She catches a glimpse of dank bricks in a wall; a view from a tube train hurtling into a bend of a tunnel . . . The train turns the corner and rattles on in the dark. The moon is swallowed into cloud.

'It's getting cold,' shivers Elsie, and she sees herself for a moment as if from somewhere else, ridiculous, afloat on the open sea in a tiny boat, in what seems to be the middle of the night. But the situation is too serious to be laughed at, and it strikes her in the same moment that there is no way out. This, for once, is a situation in which she is entirely responsible for herself; there is no one there to fall back on; the chatter of her friends cleaning the corridors, the arms of her husband, cannot extend this far.

The first drops of rain sprinkle through the dark on to the heads of the women, on to the surface of the sea. It is cold. A storm is brewing. Energy change. Sea and sky spread and change together, invisible in the dark. Now the rain falls harder, splat, splat, down from empty, endless height. One after the other, heavy and separate, drops of rain plunge and explode on individual points across the water.

'As if they were being aimed . . . or is it just chance? And is it just chance that we have come and drawn to a halt at this particular point on the ocean? But it is, also, very much not mere chance that we are here. The design of things? . . . whose design?' thinks Helen. She cannot work it out.

And Elsie's voice in the dark: 'You are not alone.' She does not actually say this, but this is the effect her voice has upon Helen and Rebecca and Jane who hear her . . . we are not alone . . . therefore, together. 'Well, I suppose we had better just go on.' These are the words that Elsie speaks. The wind whisks the words away.

Around them the storm is clawing deep into the ocean, tugging waves up in tattered streams through the surface. A lone wave scatters and re-forms far out beneath the woman on the lily leaf. As Ruby rides uneasily up on its back, she hears a stumbling agitation extending over the water, ominous, like the sound of a congregation rising for the final hymn. She sinks down into the dark.

. . .

Why? Why do the four women in their tiny boat decide to pick up the oars once more and row on, away into the grip of the stormy sea?

It is evening; I am sitting at my desk in the houseboat tethered to the concrete bank . . .

'Why do they go on?' the voice of the unknown reader washes

into my solitude.

I can't see, but I suppose that in the darkness they are steering beyond the influence of a dimension.

'A dimension?'

They are breaking through a dimension of fear. They leave behind the battle for self-preservation, the obsession with the construction of the tiny shell, the barricaded life. Beyond winning or losing, they row with the flood of death into the night . . . towards the deeper splitting of power . . . the dawn crack . . . towards . . .

I am alone. My houseboat has a light on . . . the yard is dark . . . and, suddenly, my head is full of such amazing depth . . . throw reason to the wind. (How odd that one can use a phrase for years and years and not understand it!) Throw reason to the wind, it disappears . . . and dark and dark and dark and sound. The oars strike the water.

. . .

The wind throws brittle sheets of rain across the distance, drops of water explode and divide, explode and divide, tinier and tinier, pricking infinity through the dark. Waves rise up and spontaneously collapse, mountains of sodden air avalanche down from the sky into the drag of the water. In the depths a crab is wrenched from the shell in which she cowers.

'We breathe,' whispers Elsie as she rows, 'we keep going. We pull our way to the top of the wave; rest, breathe . . . and slide deep down. We keep on going.'

'Wind lashing my face, lashing my hair across my face,' says Rebecca, as the boat strains up the side of the next wave, 'wind wrapping my body, yet I am here. Up, and it is pitch dark and the long sweep down; I am still here, absolutely and completely in the dark. As if by a miracle, we are light.'

Jane pulls her oar back. 'Yes, I have let go. I have let go. I have not found him and if I did find him now . . . I would not know what to do with him. Can you believe that!' she shouts, as they reach the crest of the next wave. 'I would not know what to do with him! . . . Bury the dead and run . . . on.' They disappear down into another

134

ocean valley.

'You know,' says Helen, 'I am so wet, it is freezing cold, but I feel quite warm.'

'What?' shouts Elsie.

'Warm! I said I feel quite warm.'

'Forlorn?' shouts Jane.

'Not at all. Warm! . . . and what's more, it is all incredibly funny. Come on, wave, do your worst!' she yells. The wave towers above them, showering water into the boat and they fly up on its back with a shriek.

'It's something that happened, it's all happened before!' shouts Helen. 'Over and over, women run into the sea . . . because of our anger, because of our pain, because of our suffering.' The words turn into a song.

Rebecca is laughing. 'You are worse than me!'

'No better, no worse.

Alive, alive,

And free from curse!' sings Helen, through the dark and the torrents of rain.

The soaking women travel on and on, out into the storm and the night. And still they move along a path; an invisible path like a path across the rim of a roaring waterfall, and the elements of darkness pass over them and under them and leave them untouched.

. . .

The rain has stopped. Four wet women, resting on their oars in a tiny boat on the dark sea, are rocked. The boat creaks. Wet hair hangs down from heads bent. Then one head jerks up in the dark like a flower. Jane peers out across the ocean and watches a ray of light grow into the dark, spreading in a horizontal line, spreading in a way which is now familiar to her . . . the birth of the dawn.

Jane, pale blue dressing-gown wrapped around her body, looks up. ('Pretty girl,' I remember the cleaning women once said.) But now her face is grinning. She is grinning through the water running in droplets over her skin. And now, with the power of a woman rising, with the power of a woman rising from the sea, she reaches out to me across the dark and silent water, gaily waving aside all

135

these clouds of faltering description and all these words typed in rows across the page. 'This is me,' says Jane. She turns away, and all the words fall back, careful black upon silent white, into place.

'Look,' she says to the others. She points across the dark to the rift between the water and the air. The sea is calm. Slowly, slowly, a transparent light is fingering its way across green shadow waves. One by one, the women raise their heads and look. The bright, spinning disc of the sun lifts into view. As the sun-disc rises, it releases a succession of tiny discs skimming across the water to the boat. The golden tip of each disc feels into the pink heart of the disc ahead, splaying it open like a fan. Each fan shape, opening, reveals a drop of light. The fans extend and extend over the sea, surrounding the boat. The boat and the water move gently up and down, and the women are aware of themselves, sitting in the middle of the dawn . . . sparkling.

. . .

Light. Ruby's lily leaf swings her slowly round to face the dawning of the sun. The light plays upon her faded hair, soft but tangled after the storm. The nets of her wedding dress flutter slightly in the breeze. Her hand edges across the veins of the leaf in search of her comb. But the comb has fallen off the leaf during the storm and is now resting deep down, miles beneath her, amongst the anemones on the ocean bed. Unable to find its object, the hand retreats back under the netted fibres of the wedding garment, and Ruby is still. She stares over the ocean to the dawn; the strong light streaming towards her irritates her eyes, causing her pain. 'Pain in my eyes . . . pain.'

Often, when the end is near, the elements are kind. The breeze flaps the netting of her veil down over her face, so that the light shining into her eyes is shattered, cut up into light squares, bright when the veil is still, but blurring when it moves . . . bright and shining world becomes soft and furry world . . . distant, her eyes close. No more dark, no more light, only turning.

The sun balances, complete and open on the horizon, and casts up into the sky. Beneath it, the figure of the woman on the lily leaf crumples and topples on to her back . . . the stage death, well

136

rehearsed. Fragile body and blond hair, she lies curled in petals of white net on her thin leaf, which continues to revolve slowly on the spot. The eyes under the net open again and stare straight up into the meshy sky. High above, a few clouds drift past. The eyes search feebly for a reflection, but find none; the sky is evaporating up and up. Then a small bird, possibly a swallow, cuts the vision in two. The shadow of the swallow flicks across her face. As the bird flies on, looping through currents of air, Ruby closes her eyes for the last time.

. . .

The women in the boat had felt a tug in the tension of the surface as the sun pushed up out of the sea. It seemed then that the sun rose heavily, struggling free from the water which clung to it in thick, gluey strands of distended light. It was with mixed feelings that they watched it rise. 'As if the sea is giving birth,' thought Rebecca.

The sun strained up undaunted through hazy bands of pink air; the gluey strands relaxed and floated down to rest on the waves like the afterbirth. The morning was silent; the sun had risen without a cry.

Then, in the space between the sun and the horizon, they saw what looked like a hollow cylinder, a dazzling shaft of light boring into the sea like a well. In the centre of the well, on its spinning surface, they saw, floating . . . a lily leaf, and the lily leaf swam round slowly, travelling inward. Then the women looked at one another, incredulous; for, sitting on the leaf, they could see the figure of a woman, dressed in white, encased by the cylindrical finger of light. And Jane realised that she had seen her before, the woman out there . . . she had seen her shadow drifting across the plain in the midst of the company of many, many women under the moon in the night. But that had been days, weeks, ago. They watched as the figure keeled over on to her back and they witnessed her struggle as the nets of her wedding dress closed over her. They watched until she became tiny, a minute ornament on the vast extent of swirling ocean . . . in the distance.

. . .

137

'We must do something!' says Rebecca. She and Helen grab their oars, their bodies fall forward. Splash after splash, they dip their oars into the water; the boat creaks and edges a few feet and then another few feet across the waves towards Ruby. Jane and Elsie do not move. Now, Jane turns to Elsie and they acknowledge in each other's eyes the understanding that this attempt at rescue is futile.

'Come on!' says Helen, straining towards the sun, fired with enthusiasm. 'Come on, don't just sit there.' She prods her elbow sharply into Elsie next to her. 'Come on!' Elsie and Jane pick up their oars. The boat moves out across the flat and open sea, heavily at first, but seeming to lighten as the pace of the oars quickens into a bending rhythm; heads to knees, heads to knees, heads to knees. When the tips of the blades touch up from the water, they leave brief marks on the green surface like the delicate footprints of a long-legged creature stalking the sun through the morning dew. Beneath them slim fish dart away, as the shadow of the boat passes overhead; behind them the footprints made by the oars smear together to form a single trail.

Every now and again, the women pause as they row, and lift their heads to judge the distance. Ruby, a little white undulation on the long line of the horizon, lies caught beneath the spotlight from the sun. They have to turn their heads to see her; they turn back and, as they lean into the next stroke, they catch a glimpse of the mist hovering over the land they have left behind, far away, like the condensation on the rim of a lens. The distance is vast; the distance both ahead of them and behind them is vast and empty. It strikes Elsie that all their elaborate swaying activity is only creating the illusion of progress. In fact, it seems to her that they are hardly moving at all; as if a string were secretly attached to the bottom of the boat, securing it to a rock on the ocean floor, and that someone was tugging on the string from below. The boat floats a little this way, a little that, controlled by tight tugs like a kite.

The sun is quick to find its heat this morning. It pumps itself up into the blue sky frantically employed in throwing hot light down on to the sea, indiscriminately, in bucketfuls. The heat speckles finely about the women in the boat and the heat speckles down on to the white net covering the still form on the lily leaf and plays there; soft

138

light on a snowy cradle which will not melt.

Sweat is beginning to gather on the foreheads of the women; it runs down Elsie's face first, tickling down the wrinkles in her skin and falling 'plop' into her lap. The sunlight in Rebecca's hair burns with a furious energy; with every backward sweep of her oar, she flings it back over her shoulder and casts a glance like a shriek towards the woman on the leaf. She jabs her oar deeper into the water and pulls back quickly, struggling to break the established rhythm and increase the speed.

Helen moves back and forth automatically with her oar. Her eyes are almost closed. The tick-tock motion of her body clears a space in her mind, into which a small, insistent thought uncoils with the threatening ease of cold, white flame; growing, taking possession, then opening into a sickening realisation. She opens her eyes, looks at the others, and sees that her realisation is shared. For a while they say nothing, and the thought flickers between them; there, not there, there . . . resiliently gaining ground until it is undeniably present; there, burning a cold, empty hole in the centre of this world of yellow light.

'We are not getting any closer to her,' says Helen. The thought is spoken. The oars drag to a halt and dangle limply into the waves. Rebecca and Jane heave their bodies round on the bench to face the others, then all four women drop forward exhausted, as if the hand with the string under the water has let go suddenly, taking the life from puppets.

The sea carries on without them, flowing out and out, gently gathering gold threads into green, towards the pink edge of the sky . . . and rests in the distance, under the sun, richly embroidered, green and golden, like the cloth upon an altar. A single branch of sunlight lingers on the centre of the cloth, about the still form of the woman curled on the open leaf, developing a circle space around her. The circle space is as fragile and quiet as the space that exists in a glass of champagne into which a finger has been inserted during a moment of abstraction, amid the murmur of wedding festivities. The leaf floats suspended on the space, bearing the body of the woman, shining like a jewel, wrapped in white, on a cloth of gold. The sun lifts easily through the sky, and, suddenly, as if the finger has been withdrawn from the glass, the shaft of light leaves the surface and vanishes above. A small wave collects at the rim of the circle space and, rolling inwards, erases the lily leaf and the woman completely . . . The sea lies flat and calm.

Slowly, Helen sits up from the slumped position in which she has been resting, head pressed down on to the points of her knees, damp dark, hot and aching. The weight of heat, which has accumulated on top of her, slides down her back. She straightens her shoulders and lifts her head. Dizzy sun is burning dry and white. Rebecca, Elsie and Jane are motionless, heads down; their hair has fallen together in bunches, auburn, grey and brown, in the cramped space in the middle of the boat. The sun drenches their hair with dry light. Helen slips her hands under her thighs on the wooden seat to support herself; her eyes start to scan the horizon for the lily leaf. She looks out steadily at first, then her head moves more quickly, slightly frantic. The other women sit up and look as well. They search the flat horizon in silence.

'She's gone,' says Jane at last.

Silence.

'Is this a death?' Helen turns to me indignantly, eyes angry, suppressing pain. Before I can answer: I didn't know, I didn't know what was going to happen . . . she turns away. Her face moves towards me, like a fish in a tank, to shoot an accusing glance and disappears.

Now, Jane is gazing down at her shoe. She grinds her toe around on the bottom of the boat; the boards are gritty with sand. She looks at Elsie. Elsie is staring into the distance at the thin horizontal line which divides the sea and the sky; her grey hair is blown back by the breeze, her face noble like a figurehead. Rebecca is silent, incredulous, silent.

Elsie, continuing to stare, starts to speak. She is speaking to no one in particular, mouthing words monotonously like sobs: 'Poor thing, poor thing . . . she wasn't even born . . . it happened before she was born. Perhaps it is for the best, perhaps it is for the best; it's a hard world. There was nothing we could do, she was gone before we got to her . . . she didn't know we were coming, how could she? . . . Poor thing, all alone out on the water . . . all alone for such a long time. Perhaps others have passed this way in the dark . . . but she was so small . . . they wrapped her in a blanket and took her away. They took her away before she was born.'

'Elsie, Elsie,' Jane is shaking her arm.

Elsie turns towards her. 'Sorry, love.'

'What is it?'

'Nothing, love . . . a child I saw once, a little girl, and it was somehow just . . . it was somehow just like . . .'

Silence.

'Well, perhaps she has gone somewhere else,' ventures Helen, 'she might have done, mightn't she? . . . People do disappear . . .'

'Do they?' says Elsie, unconvinced. 'Do people disappear?' She peers out to the point where the watery horizon vanishes into the mist covering the land. She screws up her eyes, unconsciously gripping her hands tight around the side of the boat. She is quite still, concentrating on the point, establishing a connection with it to a point inside herself . . . a point of departure. Then, very slowly and methodically, her eyes follow the silver-grey line which separates the sea from the sky, following the line like the path of a voyage along the edge of the world. As she continues to look along the line, she notices that the line is not quite rigid, not quite straight, but that it is flowing in the form of a curve, and Elsie feels as if she is flowing, too; round with the line, out along the silver horizon under the sky, round, round the world to the point where again there is mist on the land. The round line stops like a cut. She turns to face Rebecca and Jane, clear pain in her eyes. 'She's gone,' she says, 'as if she didn't exist.'

The women are silent. Waves slap nonchalantly against the sides of the boat, flapping and sagging, erasing each other: perpetual, pointless, indifferent. The sun spins up and up, ecstatic in flight . . . away from them, towards midday. The sea draws over herself a single mantle of sombre green and is quiet. A bird passes easily through the sky high above them, heading for the land.

'Elsie,' whispers Jane, 'it wasn't any good for her out there . . . cast adrift. We didn't have a chance . . . too far away . . . I mean . . .' She watches her words trail off and melt transparently into the waves. She watches them, knowing her power of speech is deserting her . . . again, lonely again, empty again, empty again . . . slap the waves . . . Jane lost again, lost again Jane. Looking down into the water, she sees the cold shape of a forgotten terror surfacing steadily. The shape is a body, her own, swathed in the pale blue dressing-gown. The face, dead, floating in hair, staring vaguely, staring up from a window in a hospital. The face looms closer to the surface. The water lapping over it clarifies the vagueness of expression in the eyes, until they communicate with a terrible silent urgency . . . pain, pain, pain. The reflection catches her into a magnetic, sucking tension. The fierce pain in the eyes strengthens; is unbearable, willing her down into the oblivion of the sea, the soft nothing world of the hospital . . . if she slips a fraction, it will be done. Then, the face in the water jerks to one side and sinks abruptly. Jane watches the shadow body swim swiftly away into the sombre depths.

'When the whales are far out at sea, they sing to each other,' says Helen.

Jane leans towards Elsie and puts her hand on hers. 'What?' she says to Helen.

'Oh, nothing,' says Helen. Seeing Jane and Elsie, she feels that what she has said is out of place, insensitive, irrelevant.

'No, what did you say?' says Jane.

'Just something I read somewhere once about whales, off the coast of America, I think. For three months of the year they leave the coast where they feed and when they are far out at sea they sing to each other . . . Sorry, I don't know why I said it really,' she adds.

They stare out across the sea in silence, the straight paths from each separate point of view spreading over the green waves at an angle of ninety degrees, like the rays from a compass. They remind me of those drawings of the four winds which you sometimes find in the corner of old maps. The sea swirls slowly about them, conjuring up visions of whales surging through the depths singing to each other, rising gently to the surface to spout water and curving back down . . . and the sound of their songs, ancient before time . . .

'And women also,' thinks Jane, 'women also, forgoing food, singing to one another far out at sea.'

Suddenly Rebecca is aware of the sun, close, boring with

142

blistering intimacy through the material of her T-shirt at the back of her neck. But when she looks up, the sun speeds away ahead of her glance and now it is there, high in the sky, spinning contentedly, ignoring her completely. The blistering sensation continues inside; she feels irritable and confined, longing for land. This feeling of irritation had started when the woman on the lily leaf had disappeared. The event had made her angry, the sort of irrational anger you feel when you recognise a friend in the street and risk your life crossing the road through the rush hour traffic, then realise, just in time, that this person is not the person you thought they were, but someone you don't know at all . . . you are angry with the stranger for not being the friend. That is how she feels about the woman on the lily leaf, that kind of feeling, only worse. It is all complicated by her awareness that anger is the last thing she should be feeling; the woman was innocent, her situation sad, tragic even, but she, Rebecca, is angry, hot and hungry.

'I'm not a bloody whale,' she thinks. Jane's hand on Elsie's hand annoys her, Helen's approval of this . . . this attitude, this pose, annoys her. And the woman on the lily leaf, the woman who might not have been a woman anyway . . . the woman who had simply vanished, vanished when they had tried so hard to reach her . . . 'Let's go,' she says, suddenly.

Jane removes her hand from Elsie's hand, quickly. 'Yes, I suppose we had better,' she replies.

The morning mist has evaporated off the land and now the women can see the frail, white coastline, far, far away across the sea. Their bodies are tired, hot and aching. When they take hold of the oars once more they seem very cumbersome and heavy. The sun is shining callously down on to them from above, the waves are placid and uncaring, the land is home . . . distant hope.

The tiny boat begins to limp awkwardly across the expanse of water, up one wave and down, up the next and down, up and down. Elsie finds it hard to concentrate; she stares at the spot where the woman might have disappeared, she misses her stroke, might have . . . she is no longer sure. Around them the distance has whipped one bit of sea into another bit of sea, so that the place where the woman and the lily leaf had been is no longer distinguishable . . .

might never have been there . . . 'But she was,' Elsie reassures herself.

Helen and Jane strain on the oars, until a rhythm is established into which they can unwind their tiredness and think of nothing in particular, moving slowly across the sea from one spot to another. Now they are moving, there is a breeze. Rebecca feels better. The oars flow and relax in and out of the water with the automatic confidence of breathing, and she experiences the thrill, the stride, the strength of movement. Something horrible had happened. It occurs to her, as they strike forward towards the land, that somehow what they had seen had all been bound up with the opposite of movement: non-movement, stasis, vulnerability . . . sickly stasis, green and silver, that gluey dawn. But to Elsie, it seems that they are carrying with them the grains of a secret. Yes, there on the wooden floor of the boat lies the trace of a sea secret, wet salt grains which dry and crystallise slowly, perhaps? . . . no, she isn't sure.

High in the sky the sun reaches up to touch midday and tumbles away. It seems more well disposed to them now, less ready to shower them indiscriminately with burning waste. Instead, it occupies itself in adorning the waves with sparkling edges, offering the boat a shining path across the sea; attentive like a hostess, making ready.

'Home,' thinks Jane, picturing the beach, the crack, the grassy bank beneath the tree. It is all there, she knows it is all there . . . they left, they return, and it will all still be there. The women travel on, mostly in silence. Occasionally, they speak: 'Nearly there.' 'You OK?' 'Not long now.' The oars splash nimbly through the water, sinking echoes into the depths.

The sun floats down amongst islands of cloud, orange and blue, and vanishes behind the mountains. Shortly afterwards, the women pull the boat on to the shore in the twilight.

It takes every ounce of energy they have left to drag the boat up the shingle.

'Shall we turn it over again?' says Elsie.

The heave it on to its side and let it down on to its belly in several co-ordinated movements as it they were turning a patient over in her hospital bed. The boat sinks down thankfully on to the stones clasping her shadow to her stomach. The women walk away in the semidarkness, making a loud crunching sound on the shingle. They climb the slope and now they are prowling along the shoulder of the ridge, one behind the other. And creeping towards them comes a dot, a blacker than black dot, padding silently on four paws . . . comes the cat, with her tail held high. She stops. Jane, the second figure in the line, breaks rank and runs towards her . . . she crouches down and picks her up. The women turn towards the plain, pause, and disappear down the other side of the ridge. Darkness falls.

SECTION 17
Birthday

It is May, the month of my birthday. When I wake in the mornings now, I am not cold . I go back to sleep. I wake again and peer up over the covers. I follow the two straight lines of my legs, stretched in front of me under the blankets, along the length of my bed to the end. There is no one beside me; I take in this fact, sometimes gratefully, sometimes sadly.

My boat sways. I hear the wind blowing outside, whisking over the surface of the water. I hear the splashes, the gurgles, the slops: fish, swans and ducks, jump, swim and sail by. The ducks quack loudly.

As I do not bother to draw the curtain which separates the bedroom and the sitting-room before I go to bed anymore, when I wake I can see into the sitting-room. At the end of the bed, with its back to me, stands the stove, black iron pipe of a chimney held straight up to the ceiling like the long tail of an animal. My armchair is beside the stove, dark red painted wood, flaking green whicker seat. The sides of the room are obscured by the clumps of curtain, but I can see the edge of the sideboard with its lace cloth, a bit of the record player. Facing my chair, at a reasonable distance, sits the empty visitor's chair. Two purple-papered walls partition the end of the sitting-room; they do not meet. A shelf runs across each wall from which the limbs of plants suspend and curve towards the windows, like tangled green hair either side of a parting. The vertical parting in the middle is the flap of a dark red curtain shielding the entrance to my writing room beyond. A crack.

The boat rocks; the sitting-room is rocked and is still. The contents of the room are not yet solid, they are still half-submerged in shadows from the night. Blank and empty. And now the light . . . pale light flickers on to the white, shiny ceiling and runs between

146

the painted beams. It settles gently on to the thin white carpet on the floor. It falls in a simple line, silvery, along the wooden arms of the visitor's chair and gathers on the round wooden curves at the end of the arms held tight like knuckles; it coaxes life.

A stir in my armchair. The black and white face of my cat springs into view; we regard each other with expressions of alert incredulity; surprised we are, to find each other here. Then she remembers that, although on the boat in the morning one could wake to find oneself anywhere . . . although it is quite possible for everything to change overnight . . . generally, it doesn't. She leaps on to the bed and pads carefully along the ridges of my legs, her face growing larger and larger as I look; she greets me with a nudge against my cheek.

The radio is on, the news drones forth. I sit in my armchair eating my toast. At length I get up, return the breakfast tray to the kitchen and switch off the radio. I gather my blue folder, my pen, my ashtray and tobacco; I cross the sitting-room with these objects bulging out under my arm. I draw back the curtain and climb the steps into my writing room. Desk, chair, rug, plant. I arrange my objects on the desk, pick up my pen and begin to pore over pages of black scribble . . .

'Why are you telling me all this now?' calls the voice of the unknown reader, soft woman's voice.

Well, I'm trying to bring it all together, tying up the threads, re-establishing a point of contact, completing the shape . . . you know, reaching for a conclusion. The pen is very heavy. I'm looking for an end! I cry out in desperation.

'I thought so,' the voice sighs, bored.

But I do want to tell you about the month of May on the boat, and the leaves and the flowers on the horse chestnut trees across the river, the numbers of birds – there are so many more now . . . and look, the sun, the sun . . . I am tugging at an invisible arm; she is gone. Actually, it is rather grey outside; not raining, but certainly not sunny as I would have contrived. A woman is walking under the trees on the other side . . . perhaps she is you? or you are she? She wanders round the corner . . . No.

I lock up the boat and hurry through the town. The streets are swollen, full of pushing people. They point to bright objects in shop windows, their eyes flare, they jab at each other with their elbows, they carry bags stuffed with things, they laugh, they chatter. Their sound is a buzz, it is a language I hardly understand. I balance along the kerb, I feel I am invisible. Perhaps this is the next step . . . perhaps houses, shops, children, washing lines, noise . . . How do I transfer all this to the plain? . . . A white fluffy form brushes against my ankles; I watch it being led away . . . dogs on leads? No.

The railway cafeteria is dirty. I take my cup of tea to a table in a dingy corner, where an elderly woman is sitting. She smells of lavender . . . the old woman? But here is the train, I rise and leave through the glass swing doors, which are smeary with smoke and steam. She tastes her tea and, sipping, smiles sagaciously.

. . .

I am sitting in an empty railway carriage. The train pulls out of the station. Quicker and quicker, the sunlight sprints across square roofs. I watch as house follows house follows tree follows house . . .

'What about Mr Smith-god and Mr Jones?' enquires the woman sitting opposite me, softly.

Oh, that's easy, their fate is clear . . . outside, look . . . for there they stand at the foot of a lawn, they wear beige cardigans . . . in the end they will die . . . I, I watch her. She does not look up; in silence she stares into her book, then raises a hand as if to wave. Out of the window, a bicycle is racing us, its rider's clothes flapping russet and green, red hair flying in the wind. The bicycle slows down, we draw away, again house follows tree follows house. In the empty carriage she turns the final page, a jolt into a dark tunnel. Dark . . . I follow a thin gleam travelling on the wall, which shapes a smile and beside it a hand ready to wave. I must concentrate. Focus the smile and then the wave. My hand flickers up, lonely, and the reflection is smashed by a screech. The train stops. The carriage is empty . . . everywhere, the glare of bright station lights. The door. I must push the door open. Slide down the window, reach out for the handle, the handle on the outside, awkward to turn, now push the door . . . open.

148

. . .

The door swings shut; a damp chill is oozing into the boat. I do not take off my coat or switch on the light, I sit in my chair . . . I must write quickly, now that I know who I am.

The hunched wave breaks the reflection, carries the curtains into the dark. I know that I am Ruby. I must write quickly now, I must be brave, now that I know who I am.

The hunched wave walks away, dragging the houseboat across the sea on a string . . . I am Ruby, I am bright, I am brilliant. I am Ruby . . . crying in the dark. Endless, open, endless dark. Breeze cool. No time, little time . . . Messages on paper floating, swirl.

Be brave Ruby . . . Ruby. Voices in the dark . . . I turn away. I turn and spin. And I know, I am all, all the voices, present, past, future, turning to the dark . . . and watching, from a distance I watch.

Light. Ah. By day they come. Women. I see who I have been, will be. I look at myself. A window. I stare back from a window, always I watch, all ways . . . I comb my hair. It is a square window, a mirror; I stare, I wave.

The sky is empty, open; I stare, I wave . . . up there . . . a tree, blossom bursts, I shout out for joy, beautiful, beautiful shining. But deep sea rocking . . . I shout, I smile, I wave . . . No time . . . write.

Beam of light through the dark. I am Jane. I was Jane escaping . . . I run round, round, round the path, I run . . . Doctors, nurses, pursuing, follow . . . Ah, the road, screech . . . headlights, hand in the dark. Drag me back, sobbing bundle, sitting by the window in the dark.

Ha, what's this? a stir? a tap? . . . Tapping on the water . . . Voices? No . . . 'Can you see her?' women say. Rescue! I scream, I

149

smile, I wave, I turn, no . . . I must write it down. I must write quickly. A rowing boat tapping at the water in the dark. A storm, a squall . . .

Into the dark I stare, into my face rocking in the water. Light, dark . . . snatches, tatters. I veer into a tunnel, sharply . . . Out, under the moon, I reflect myself in her; Elsie, mother . . . tender light treading through the dark. Mother . . . my mother is cold and thinks me charming . . . In the beginning the light comes flowing . . . in the beginning, yes, it flowed. Who am I? I am Ruby, I must write quickly . . .

Voices. Always voices. 'Can you see her . . . a woman tossing in a storm?' I turn, waves splash, water gurgles . . . why so furious? shattering the dark.

Light. Sudden light on water . . . I sparkle, I dazzle, actress, queen . . . I will write quickly. I must be calm. See. See how I have strewn the surface of the sea with pages? Messages, over the ocean floating out. I am Ruby . . . I reflect. In windows, water, tunnels, I . . . I must write quickly, I will be calm.

Light is too bright . . . Sun, sky, sky, I . . . I see no more. Not so, I see through squares. I peer through crevices, I see through chinks. 'What is she doing?' always a voice. All ways. Women looking for me. I see them riding past, high on the watery crest, they, they heave away. I see them through my chinks of light. I must write quickly . . . I watch them go. They were looking for me . . .

My pen, ha . . . My pen is gone . . . sinking . . . Now, talk . . . I have a voice, it was never heard.

Turning, turning . . . I turn . . . rough waves pushing, round and round. I cling tight, tight to the leaf, in wind which spins . . . and, look, I discover her. I was Helen, under a sheet and here beneath a leaf . . . I see a tree, and what's this? Singing . . . No, I am Ruby, I must talk quickly . . .

And the bearing light . . . the heavy beam . . . Now, high, a bird flaps and flaps . . . a line to the land. To the land . . . no longer light . . . no longer dark . . . turning, swirling . . . lost . . . I must . . . talk . . . Yes . . . this is . . . my voice . . . two waves, gentle . . . rising . . . water over . . . dark, light, I . . . no longer . . . I . . .

. . .

I sling down my bicycle at the front of the house and run upstairs. I unlock the door, I hang up my jacket on a peg, I hurry along the hall, peering in, smelling the old smell of still rooms. I have arrived. I have come back to the white room at the end of the corridor, with brightness in my clothes. I didn't like that gluey dawn and now, in my white studio, I want clear colours, red and yellow, nasturtium colours. So, I dismantle the easel and carry the abandoned canvas into another room, making ready. After a cup of coffee, I come back.

I crouch, I breathe in deeply, I dip my brush into gold and, suddenly, it flows, and all the way around the room, from wall to wall, I paint a line of dripping gold. I stand back, and now I paint the green and gentle rolling sea and the yellow, ever-hopeful undulation of the land. And so, by nightfall, the walls are colourful and are no longer walls at all. When the moon shines through the skylight and washes the earth with silver, I hear our voices whisper.

My friends come to visit me bringing bunches of flowers. I make tea; we eat apples and cake, sitting on the floor, laughing. We work hard, we keep on discussing the work in progress, going for walks, and we are learning to touch the vibrant green ferns. At night I sleep beneath the spreading branches of the tree beside the murmuring crack of gold and I hear choruses of voices. Oh, yes, I do! Choruses of voices proclaiming the dawn.

Morning comes flooding light; steadily, I apply colour to this space, and so the shapes of our paths emerge and spiral. I stand back to watch the growth of lilac unfolding in the bud, erupting into purple joy of mountains. A petal tinged with pink detaches itself and is borne away sadly, sadly, on the green, green sea. And I know that we exist and I know that we shall never die and I carry on, tasting the water at the birth of a spring, testing my toes on the firmness of the ground, and I dance through a wood with an extravagant sweep of the brush, sifting out bluebells.

'Ahem!' I glance over my shoulder. The boys are here with notebooks and pens. 'We are conducting an interview,' they say.

As I turn away to wipe my hands, I wonder why the sight of them there, in their grey suits, so innocuous and friendly, smiling encouragement, always produces this sinking feeling, this chaos of feeling . . . as if I were tossed into a stirring swamp of guilt and frustration; and yet, I resolve as I carefully dry my brush, and yet, it is for me also, that we will try again, that we will make the attempt to communicate. 'Oh, hello,' I say, 'come in.'

'Miss Rebecca Brown?'

'I've changed my name.'

They consult one another briefly, assessing the statement, glancing and raising their eyebrows. I continue.

'My name is now Rebecca Yellow. I change it every day, actually: Rebecca Green, Rebecca Orange, Red, Rebecca Blue and Yellow.'

'Ahem, very interesting,' says Mr Smith. 'Now, perhaps you could tell us something about your work in this room?'

I'm afraid that's done it . . . the sight of Mr Jones carefully writing down all my names: Yellow, Green, Orange, etc., in the correct order, makes me want to laugh! 'Room?' I say.

'Yes,' says Mr Smith, aggrieved but patient, 'the mural you have executed, Miss . . . er . . . what is it today?'

'I think it is Yellow,' prompts Mr Jones.

'Ah, yes. The mural which you have executed, Miss Yellow, on the walls of this room. Now do I make myself clear?'

Walls? . . . Not walls, and I certainly have not 'executed' anything and . . . calm down Rebecca, be calm . . . 'Well, I had this sort of vision of a tree and . . .'

'Excuse me, Rebecca,' says Elsie, stepping out from the 'wall' with a suitcase in her hand, 'I'm off to Spain for a holiday.' Mr Jones jumps to one side with a nervous 'Ooooh!' You know, the type of sound women are supposed to make when, seeing a mouse, they leap on to a chair . . .

'See you!' I shout to Elsie, who is already in the corridor.

'Bye, love.'

. . .

Mr Jones is anxiously nudging Mr Smith.

'Speak, Jones.'

'It's the sea! It should not be green . . . it should be blue!'

'Well, you don't get any less predictable!' says Helen, sitting under the tree. She stands up and takes Mr Jones by the hand. 'Come on, it's time for you to go back to the university, where everything is nice and grey, you'll be safer there.' She leads him away.

Mr Smith takes a step towards me. 'Now, Miss Yellow . . . I . . . er . . . my assistant, Mr Jones, made mention of a lily leaf or was it a houseboat? Some slight discrepancy there, but, nevertheless, this connection struck me at the time as rather an interesting, might I even say a "novel", idea!'

A joke . . . Mr Smith has made a joke! Yes, I know it is rather a feeble one, but still . . .

'A "novel" idea!' he repeats with a chuckle.

'As regards the lily leaf,' I say, 'things change, it had to go.'

'And the houseboat?' he asks.

'I'm here,' I reply.

Pause.

'Perhaps you could tell me what first interested you in the concept of landscape depiction? It is an old concern, one that, indeed, has taxed artistic capacity more than any other in our history . . .'

'I wanted to be able to live my life.'

'Ah ha. I see. Could we then, in a certain sense, consider your work to be constructed in the manner of a map, in which we can chart the development of a certain attitude to life and experience?'

'Yes, I suppose we could.'

'Very good. And tell me, Miss Yellow, if there were really . . .' he shifts his weight from one foot to the other and leans forward, 'I mean, if there really were, in existence, such a place, what would you call it?'

'I don't think it has got one name . . . but I think I would call it the place where our souls mingle, the place where our souls are born anew, out on the plain where . . .'

'Pardon me, whose souls?'

'Oh, come on, Rebecca!' says Jane, jumping down from the shingle ridge. Mr Smith watches us go; a woman in a blue dressing-gown and me in my red-and-green gear, smeared with bluebell paint. We walk out arm in arm.

'You can't,' he calls out after us from the top of the stairs. 'You can't go out dressed like that! You can't stroll about like that, in the street!' 'Nice pussy,' he says to the cat at his feet. 'Pussy, pussy, come here pussy.' But the cat turns her back and stalks behind us to the front door.

And it is whispered that Mr Smith stood for a long time, alone. And it is also whispered that as he stood, he thought, just for a second, mind you: he thought he heard the sound of a wave breaking on a shore. So he pulled himself together and, when we come back, he has gone.